COAST OF FEAR

ALSO BY CAROLINE CRANE

The Girls Are Missing
Summer Girl

COAST OF FEAR

A NOVEL OF SUSPENSE

Caroline Crane

DODD, MEAD & COMPANY
NEW YORK

1   2   3   4   5   6   7   8   9   10

Library of Congress Cataloging in Publication Data

Crane, Caroline.
Coast of fear.

I. Title.
PS3553.R2695C6   813'.54   80-26819
ISBN 0-396-07950-4

COAST OF FEAR

1

Using her suitcase as a wedge, Jessica Hayden maneuvered her way through a traffic snarl in front of the Gare de Lyon. A gusty wind pummeled her bags and coat, and a drop of rain splashed against her cheek.

So much for Paris. Never before had she worn a coat in July. But, if she could find her way onto the right train, within ten hours she would reach the sunny Riviera coast.

Under the vast, skylighted roof of the station, with its lacing of steel supports, the day seemed somehow brighter. Young people carrying backpacks, and older ones with suitcases, clustered around a timetable board. Setting down her own bags, she looked for her train. The 10:05 to Lyons, Marseilles, Nice, and Ventimiglia. *Voie* 19.

Nice. Written up there on the board, it took on a new reality. She thought of the phone call she must make when she arrived.

Actually, she supposed, she did not have to make it. She had written the Lanniers, they had chosen not to reply, and that was that.

Unfortunately, it was not so easily dismissed. She was not doing it for the Lanniers—not the living ones, anyway—or even for herself, but for Françoise, who was dead. And that, somehow, made the promise more binding.

In a smaller, adjoining section of the station, under another skylighted roof, she found *Voie* 19. She had almost reached the point where the track began when suddenly, in the scurrying, shifting crowd, she recognized a face.

It couldn't be. Jessica stood still. It couldn't be, she was imagining things.

But he saw her, too. And after all, why couldn't it be he? They had something in common. For an instant, as the small dark eyes met hers, she was transported back to Françoise Lannier's room in Fort Sheffield, New York.

It certainly was the same face. It had the same tight-ness, the thin, rather prominent chin, the bony nose, and creases that resembled smile lines, although she had never seen him smile.

"Weyland?" she said. And he vanished. He would not have heard her, anyway, in the hubbub of the station. He had been too startled to hide his recognition, so she knew it was Weyland, but the look he gave her was hardly one of acquaintance meeting acquaintance in a faraway land.

It had been a look of pure amazement, without a shred of pleasure. It might have been hostile, too, and wary. She could not really tell, in that brief moment, for they had both been caught off guard.

A stout woman brushed past her, dragging a suitcase on wheels. Jessica started again toward the train.

Weyland. She had met him only once. Françoise was French, but what was he, with a name like that? He spoke with an accent, yet it was indefinable. A French accent was quite definable. And what was he doing in the station? Had he just gotten off a train, or was he heading toward the same one she was taking?

A terrifying thought pushed its way into her mind. *He must have killed her.* She did not know why this occurred to her, except that he had been there shortly before it happened, and he was never fully explained. Françoise had begged her not to mention him to anyone.

But Françoise had not known she was soon to die.

Just then Jessica saw him again, walking purposefully

down another platform in the distance. She felt relieved—unaccountably, for he had nothing to do with her.

She reached her train and looked for carriage 4, second class. It was the third one she came to. Sliding her suitcase into a rack by the door, she found her reserved seat next to the window and settled down for what would be an all-day trip.

Although nearly an hour remained before departure time, the train was rapidly filling. Vaguely she wondered why half the seats in the car were turned one way and half the other. Because of this arrangement, the two seats just in front of her faced each other. They were claimed by four young girls traveling with knapsacks and bedrolls. Almost immediately the girls were ousted by a family that held reservations for the seats.

The mother of the family, a dark-haired, sad-faced picture of French middle-class respectability, wept through the window as she waved an endless good-bye to her relatives on the platform. Her three teenaged children entertained themselves by switching seats, until every possible combination had been tried several times. Outside, faint sunlight glimmered on the train on the next track and soon disappeared.

A voice spoke to her in French. Jessica looked up to see an elderly nun carrying a small valise. The words, spoken softly, had come too fast for her limited grasp of the language. The nun pointed to the seat beside her, clearly asking whether it was taken.

"Je ne sais pas," Jessica began. The problem was taken out of her hands by a man in an olive-tan suit. With a charming apology, he informed the nun that the seat was *réservée.* As she continued down the aisle, he stuffed a raincoat onto the shelf above the seat, nodded to Jessica, and sat down, holding an attaché case on his lap.

Jessica gave him a thin smile and watched uneasily until the nun found a seat at the other end of the car.

"I suppose you think I should have given it to her," said the man in a plainly American voice.

She looked at him in surprise. "How did you know I speak English?"

"The address on your luggage tag." He nodded toward the flight bag at her feet.

"You're very observant."

And very well dressed. His tan suit was expensively cut. His hair was sandy brown, and his eyes, behind glasses with pink plastic rims, were also brown. She judged him to be about thirty. And not bad-looking, except for those pink rims.

"You shouldn't put your address where everybody can see it," he told her. "People look for that at the airport, and then they go and burglarize your house."

"They wouldn't have an easy time of it," she said. "My parents are always there, it's right over our store. And we have a big German shepherd dog."

"In that case, I should imagine you're safe." He stood up, reached into a pocket of his raincoat, and took out a copy of the French news magazine L'Express.

He opened it, but did not read. Instead he watched her with a little smile of amused interest. "Where is this home of yours that's so well guarded?"

"New York," she replied.

"City?"

"No, upstate. A place called Kennersville. You wouldn't have heard of it. Where are you from?"

"Cleveland. Isn't this amazing? Two innocents abroad, and we end up with reservations right next to each other. We must have the same travel agent. Who's yours?"

"I did it myself through the French National Railroads."

"Very enterprising." He nodded his approval. "How far are you going?"

"Nice."

"That's quite a trip. I get off at Marseilles. The train goes local after Marseilles, you know, even if it doesn't show on the timetable. What are you doing in Nice? The jazz festival?"

"What jazz festival?"

"Oh, come on. You can't be going to Nice and not know about the jazz festival. It started Thursday and runs to the sixteenth. All the big bands. It's outside in a park, three different bandstands. You can walk around and choose."

"It sounds lovely." Her attention faltered as she thought again of Weyland. Why had he looked like that? Startled and hostile. He couldn't really have anything to hide. He had been gone for nearly a week when Françoise was killed.

Or perhaps he never left.

"You're not a jazz buff?" the man asked.

"I love it."

"You've got something else on your mind, I can see that. If you love jazz, maybe we could go some evening."

"I thought you were going to be in Marseilles."

"Only for tonight. It's just an evening conference. Then I get a few days' vacation. Where are you staying?"

"Wait a minute, I don't even know you."

"By the time we get to Marseilles, you'll know me. It's seven hours. But just to speed things up a little, the name's Steve Wilcox."

"Jessica Hayden."

The train began to ease forward.

"What do you do in Kennersville, Jessica?"

"At the moment, nothing. It's my address, that's all. I just finished college."

"I see. Taking a little break before the big job hunt. What about your family? You mentioned a store."

"A grocery store. They own it."

"No kidding, a real mom-and-pop store? I like that."

5

He smiled sheepishly. "I hope you don't mind all the questions. It's just that, you see, people from big cities don't really understand how people in small towns ever manage to earn a living. We figure you can't all be farmers."

"And people in small towns," she countered, "don't understand how people in big cities ever manage to survive." Through the window across the aisle, she watched the passage of an unassuming section of Paris outskirts.

Steve fumbled in his breast pocket, withdrew a pack of cigarettes, and offered her one.

"No, thanks," she replied. "I don't smoke."

"Then what are you doing in a smoking car?"

"It was the only window seat I could get."

He put a cigarette between his lips, took a thin black lighter from his pocket, flicked it a few times with no success, then reached into a different pocket for another.

"So you're not going to the jazz festival," he said. "Just a holiday?"

"I don't know what you'd call it. Sort of an errand of compassion, maybe."

It sounded sanctimonious. She tried to explain.

"I had a friend at college this year, a girl from Nice. She —just a few months ago, in April, she was killed. It was a robbery. A stupid, idiot mugging. I felt so terrible. You know, not only for her, but she was a guest in our country."

"So what are you going to do, put flowers on her grave?"

"No, actually I thought I'd give her family a call. Maybe try to see them, if they'll let me."

Her face felt hot. In an unconsciously distracting gesture, she pushed back her hair. It was the red in her red-brown hair that made her blush so easily. And, of course, it was a silly reason.

Not only silly, but conceited, to think that the formi-

6

dable Lanniers needed anything to do with her. Even Françoise had appeared to drift away from them, although never completely away from her brother Marius, whose photograph, in a silver frame, she had kept on her dresser to the very end. "You must meet him, Zhessica," she had said. "He is so-o-o 'andsome."

Steve regarded her with an odd half smile. "You came all the way to France for that?"

Another quick blush. "Of course not. I always wanted to see Europe. It's a graduation present from my parents."

"I'd say those are some pretty nice parents you have."

"Yes, they are. And it was nice that they happened to sell their house and move into the apartment over the store just when I graduated. So I have the house sale to thank for this, but I don't know if I can last the summer. Europe's more expensive than I thought."

"Those people in Nice," he said, "the girl's family. Will you be staying with them?"

"I'm not even sure they know I'm coming. I wrote a letter, but they never answered. Maybe they're away."

"Any reason why they might not want to see you?"

She flinched at the directness of his question.

"That's up to them, isn't it? They might not care at all about Françoise's American friends. Maybe they're still bitter about her death. But I'm going to call them anyway. It's just something I have to do."

"I don't think you should."

"Why not?"

His mouth twisted in a sad smile. "Just because, in case you haven't thought of it, you might be giving them even more pain. You should let them get over it. You'll be nothing but a living reminder of something they might rather forget."

"How can they forget?" she asked. "It's going to be with them the rest of their lives."

"True. But I said *living* reminder. They might resent

7

the fact that you're alive while their daughter's dead."

She had not thought of it that way. But why should they? Unless they were totally irrational—as some people were when confronted with an unacceptable loss.

The sun glimmered again, trying to push its way through the clouds.

He said, "I suppose you have something you wanted to give them? Some kind of momento, or pictures, maybe?"

"Only my sympathy."

It was true that Françoise had given her a photograph not long before her death, but Jessica intended to keep it. The family undoubtedly had many more.

"Think about what I said," he told her, and opened his magazine.

They were in the countryside now, traveling along the Seine. It was a calm, wandering river, in a setting that was green and pleasant, with grassy banks, stands of poplars, and willow trees dipping toward the water. An occasional picturesque old house of darkened stone and stucco fitted so naturally into the scenery that it almost seemed part of nature.

Steve looked up from his reading. "Are you thinking about it?"

She answered lightly, "I'm really old enough to live my own life, you know. It's good of you to be so concerned, but I honestly don't think the world will fall apart if I go and meet the family of a friend of mine."

"Not under ordinary circumstances, maybe. But there's been violence, don't forget that. And they didn't answer your letter. I would take that as a rebuff, if I were you."

"Which, fortunately, you're not. Steve, I just had an idea. Why don't we talk about something else? Tell me what you're doing here in Europe. Is it work?"

He gave a mock sigh. "Now you have me. It's work, and I only wish it were something that would touch your romantic heart, but the fact is, I'm a salesman."

"A salesman of what? And how do you know I have a romantic heart?"

"To the second question—I'm a pretty good reader of human nature, and your mission here only confirms what I read. To the first—of industrial machinery. Now doesn't that thrill you?"

"Oh, very much. I'm sure you fill an essential need."

"I certainly do. And on that note, how about some lunch? There's a cafeteria car a little way ahead."

She hesitated. "Is it all right to leave my luggage?"

"Sweetheart, who's going to steal your luggage? Where would they go with it? You're quite safe, at least until twelve-thirty, when we stop at Dijon. Come on."

It was eleven now. A little early for lunch, but he persuaded her that the train, and therefore the café car, would become more crowded later on. She followed him, lurching as the train rocked, through a first-class carriage with carpeted floors and spacious, upholstered seats, then through another that was divided into compartments.

"I thought all the cars on European trains would have compartments," she remarked as she stumbled after him.

"Disappointed?" He turned to smile at her. "It's too bad we can't give you the Orient Express with all that pre-war Agatha Christie opulence. Probably your whole impression of European trains is based on the movies."

"Of course," she answered coldly. "Isn't their whole impression of us based on the movies?"

"Touché." He slid open the door to the cafeteria car. "I really didn't mean to be patronizing."

Whether he meant to be or not, he was. Still, if she were to meet the Lanniers, they would probably be ten times as patronizing, for they came from a background that was secure in its wealth and sophistication. To them, she would be only a small-town hick from barbarian America. Maybe Steve was right, she ought to forget the whole thing.

"Hang on," he said as he handed her a tray. "This is a bit tricky on a moving train."

The car really was a tiny, complete cafeteria, with food that looked surprisingly good for the cramped circumstances. But then, this was France. Jessica selected a small, neatly decorated salad of pickled beets, a hot plate of pork chops and fried potatoes, and a chocolate éclair. They shared a bottle of red wine. It was far more lunch than she would have eaten at home, but it would probably have to last her most of the day.

Steve asked, "How long are you planning to stay in Nice?"

"I have my hotel for a week," she said. "If I decide to stay longer, I'll have to find something cheaper."

"Don't stay longer. There's a lot more to Europe than Nice."

"I know that. But I have all summer."

"I think you might love Vienna. And Salzburg."

"I'll get there."

"Rome. Sorrento."

"I hadn't planned on Sorrento."

He was shocked. "You'd miss Capri? Pompeii?"

"Oh, well, if you insist."

They returned to their own car, and she watched the countryside become more hilly as the train approached Dijon. Somewhere, not far away, were the Alps. She saw one or two mountains in the distance that began to look somewhat imposing, but the real Alps would come later in the summer.

After Dijon she slept for a while. When she opened her eyes, they were traveling beside a vineyard.

"I didn't mean to sleep," she told Steve. "I really don't want to miss anything. It must have been the wine."

"You didn't miss anything except maybe a few sheep." He retrieved her purse from the floor where it had fallen.

"If you're so blasé about all this," she said, "why are

you taking the train? Why didn't you fly and get it over with?"

"And miss the chance to sit next to a pretty girl for seven hours?"

"There might be prettier girls on a plane." She combed her hair and powdered the shine on her nose. The plane, she knew, was very expensive. Perhaps his company wouldn't pay for it.

"I doubt it," he said in answer to her comment. "I like your kind of looks. There's a freshness about you. You're unspoiled, natural."

"Please don't tell me I'm fresh scrubbed and healthy looking. And I do have on eye makeup. That's not natural."

"Okay, I won't tell you you're fresh scrubbed and healthy looking. But I like it, whatever it is."

His compliments made her wary. They sounded like a prelude to something she preferred to avoid, at least for now. But he backed off and lapsed into a comfortable silence.

As they traveled deeper into the south of France, the earth became dry, white, and rocky. Pine trees gave it a bristly appearance, and Jessica saw her first Mediterranean umbrella pines with their mushroom-shaped tops. By now, the sun was shining clearly.

Again she thought of the Lanniers. What if they hadn't gotten her letter? When she telephoned, they would not know who she was. It would take so much explaining. Or they might know who she was and still not want to see her.

Steve was slipping the magazine into his attaché case. He had not read much of it. They had spent the time talking, mostly about her. She wondered how he always managed to steer the conversation away from himself.

Outside the window, a high mass of rock appeared to block the way into Marseilles. She watched it, an unfolding scene of fantastic white formations, strange shapes, whirls, and diagonals.

With a roar they entered a tunnel that went on forever, straight through the mountain. A world of blackness. Beside her, Steve clicked his attaché case closed. She felt him leaning toward her. He said, "You never told me where you're staying."

"Hotel Foster. I can't remember the address."

"I'll find it."

They burst out of the tunnel into sunny Marseilles. Or at least into a sunny railroad yard, which was all she could see from the train.

Steve said, "I'll call you tomorrow when I get to Nice." He pushed his way toward the door through the crowds of young people who had overflowed the seats and were sitting on the floor at the end of the car. One held a small shaggy dog on his lap. Jessica heard voices speaking in English and saw an American couple passing a wine bottle back and forth.

A middle-aged man who smelled of garlic sat down in the seat beside her. She squeezed away from him, hoping he would not try to talk, and concentrated on the window. Steve was nowhere in sight.

She glanced at her watch. After seven hours, the train had not lost a minute. It had reached Marseilles at 5:14, or, in French time, 17:14, exactly as the timetable stated. She could not imagine any train at home, even on the short run from Albany to Kennersville, being so prompt.

After a lengthy wait, but again no longer than was specified in the timetable, the train began to back up. It picked up speed and continued backing. The rock formations she had seen earlier gave way to new ones. By the time they had traveled several kilometers, she grasped the fact that she would be riding backward all the way to Nice. Now she understood the reason for half the seats facing one way and half the other. She had not felt the slightest bump at

12

Marseilles as they coupled an engine onto what, until then, had been the rear of the train.

Soon she caught a glimpse of the Mediterranean itself. Besides the umbrella pines, there were date palms. With so much variety in the space of about five hundred miles, it was no wonder the French thought their country had everything.

As Steve had said, the train became a local, stopping at Toulon, Fréjus, and then still more frequently, at Cannes, Juan-les-Pins, Antibes. She was beginning to feel hungry, but it did not worry her. She knew they would reach Nice on time, at exactly 20:13.

And at 8:13 by her watch, they did reach Nice. The garlic man had gone. At Cannes, she thought. The train was half empty. It was nearing the end of its run. She slung her flight bag over one shoulder, her long-strapped purse over the other, and collected her suitcase from its rack near the door.

And then she was outside in the warm late day, trying to get her bearings. The station, it seemed, was below the platform. She would have to go downstairs to reach the street and a taxi. As she started toward the exit, she caught a glimpse of broad shoulders and a wide head disappearing down the stairwell.

And she knew, without a doubt, that it was Weyland.

2

Her hotel room was modest, clean, and blue. Even the bathroom fixtures were blue. A floor-length window looked out over a back alleyway and into the leaves of a tree. She pulled a chair close to the window and, in a soft breeze, sat contemplating the gathering dusk.

She thought of Weyland. It had been a shock, discovering he was on the same train. Probably he lived here in Nice, and that was how he knew Françoise. But the same train?

No, what really bothered her was the way he had looked at her back there in Paris. *He* had been the one who was shocked. It was not a reaction she would have expected. She could not help wondering what caused it and was especially suspicious, since murder was involved.

But maybe that was all it was—the thought of Françoise, and suddenly seeing Jessica, who reminded him of Françoise the last time he saw her. He must have loved her. Poor Weyland.

Beside her bed was a telephone, and a directory on the shelf below it. She had already looked them up. *Lannier, Marius,* at the address she knew had been Françoise's.

She had, at one point, picked up the phone, then put it back. After all, they had not answered her letter. There could have been many explanations for that. Perhaps they never received it, or had been away, or had answered and the reply never reached her.

Or perhaps they wanted nothing to do with her.

But she had promised herself she would call.

Later, she thought. *Later.* She would go out and look around first, while it was still early. And certainly have some dinner. She had not eaten since lunch on the train.

Locking the heavy wooden shutters, for her window was only three floors above the alley and much too accessible to that tree, she walked down several flights of stairs, rather than wait for the small, creaking elevator.

At the desk she picked up a sketchy map of downtown Nice. She started out toward the Promenade des Anglais, which ran along the beachfront. It was the only part of Nice that she knew by name.

She had walked two blocks when, off to her left, the narrow street opened into a busy, brightly lit pedestrian area. There were stores of all kinds, small hotels, and a multitude of outdoor cafés. She paused in front of one whose façade was plastered with signboards offering thirty kinds of pizza.

It was crowded, both inside and out. She started to turn away, when one of the outdoor tables became vacant. After she sat down, it was nearly fifteen minutes before a harried waiter came to clear and reset it for her. He shoved a menu into her hand and disappeared, returning ten minutes later to take her order.

The delay did not disturb her. It was obvious that he was busy, and she found her appetite considerably dulled as she thought of the Lanniers only a phone call away. She had not expected to be intimidated, but they were French, wealthy, and far outside her usual range of experience.

She waited again, this time to be served, and watched the passersby. Young couples strolled with their arms around each other. Married couples walked with their children and dogs. There were tourists with cameras, a black-haired young woman in a transparent blouse, and

15

motorcycles weaving dangerously through the crowd. From time to time a pair of gendarmes would walk by, keeping an eye on things.

At last her dinner arrived, pizza topped with fried onions and tomatoes, and a small bottle of red wine. She recalled her mother's parting advice: "Now don't forget to eat properly. You know how girls are when they go off alone, nothing but pizzas, Coke, and hamburgers."

Merta Hayden was a well-rounded woman, probably as a result of following her own advice, although Jessica doubted that she had ever gone off alone to eat. Merta's whole life so far had been spent within a hundred miles of Kennersville. She was a comfortable soul with little curiosity and even less desire for change. Her universe was "the business," her home, her husband Eddie, and Jessica, her only daughter.

Swallowing the last of her wine, Jessica felt a pang of homesickness, not for home, but for her family. They had been sweet to give her this trip. Europe meant nothing to them, but they knew how badly she wanted to see it. Her father had even insisted upon paying a little more so that she could stay at decent hotels, as he put it, with adequate security and a bathroom of her own, instead of "them fleabag places."

She could still see them, smiling and weeping and waving her off at the airport. She signaled for the check and, while she waited, took out her wallet and opened it to the picture of them standing with their arms across one another's shoulders in front of Hayden's Grocery, its windows stacked with cans of Green Giant peas and boxes of Brillo.

In the next plastic pocket was the snapshot Françoise had given her. It showed Françoise clearly, her delicate features and her eyes, which looked black although they were actually blue. The man beside her was less distinct.

16

Dark hair, thin mustache, his face in shadow, half gazing at the ground. She had asked who he was. "It doesn't matter," Françoise had said. "Just keep the picture. Put it in the wallet with your others."

It was a Polaroid shot and Françoise had cropped it to wallet size, leaving only the white border at the top. "Take it with you to Europe," she had added, "so my picture goes to Nice even if I don't." She had decided to remain in the United States for the summer. Now her wish to have the picture visit Nice took on a new poignancy.

Suddenly Jessica's chair was given a bump that almost knocked her over. She turned quickly to see the backs of three men squeezing past among the closely packed tables. She thought one of them said "Sorry" with a French accent, but could not be certain. Still, it left her gaping after them. How would they know enough to speak English to her?

She had only imagined it. None of them was Weyland, she felt sure of that. The waiter rushed by, dropped her check on the table and, after another lengthy interval, came back to collect her money.

Leaving the café, she walked the length of the pedestrian mall. It ran for several blocks and offered everything from souvenir shops to expensive-looking boutiques, all closed for the night, as well as countless eating places. She would come again when the stores were open. Now it was late—perhaps too late to call the Lanniers.

But if she waited until morning, or afternoon, they might not be there. And on the Mediterranean, people lived in the evening, when it was cooler. They would not yet be asleep.

It was almost eleven when she reached her hotel. An unheard-of time to be calling anyone. What if they didn't speak English? Her French was not up to conversational level. But the wine had dulled some of her misgivings and she must do it now. Unlocking her room, she opened the

17

shutters, looked up the number once more, and put through her call.

The phone rang four times and a man's voice answered. Jessica discovered that she could scarcely remember any French at all.

Carefully she formed the words: "Good evening, may I please speak with Madame or Monsieur Lannier? My name is Jessica Hayden. I am from the United States."

The man asked in French-accented English, "Are you calling from the United States?"

"No," she said, gratefully switching to her own language. "I'm in Nice, at the Hotel Foster, but I've *come* from the United States. Is—Madame Lannier—there?"

"Yes, she is here," replied the voice. "I am Marius Lannier. What do you want?"

The face in the silver-framed photograph. And rude, too, although perhaps that was only because of the unfamiliar language.

"I wrote you a letter," Jessica explained. "Or rather, I wrote to your mother. I don't know if she got it. I was in school with your sister Françoise. She was a very good friend of mine. I thought, since I was coming to Nice, that I'd like to meet Françoise's family, if you have the time."

There was a pause, and she waited, her heart thudding. He would ask what purpose it would serve for them to meet.

"One minute, please," he said. "Here is my mother."

A woman's voice came onto the phone. Jessica repeated her speech.

The woman said, "You are very kind to think of us." Her breath seemed to catch, and she added, "It is late now."

"Oh, I didn't mean now," Jessica hastily explained. "Maybe tomorrow—or sometime?"

"Please wait a moment."

Low voices conferred. A hand must have been placed over the receiver. Then Madame Lannier said, "Tomorrow is a good time. That is Sunday, yes?"

18

"Oh, yes, wonderful. Any time?"

Madame Lannier added something about eight o'clock, and then hung up. Jessica was left not knowing whether they meant she was to go to their house at eight o'clock, or whether they would come to her hotel. She felt too foolish to call back and ask.

She would phone them tomorrow. It would be as well to confirm the date.

After getting into bed, she lay awake for a long time, wondering what it would be like. Wondering what *they* would be like. She turned on the light and again studied the photograph of Françoise.

It was odd to have that unidentified man in the picture. She might at least have given Jessica one of herself alone. Certainly it wasn't Marius. Or Weyland. Françoise, in blue jeans and the red jacket she always wore, stared stonily at the camera, but Jessica had known her as a warm, vital person whose idealism was boundless. Her only care, Françoise had maintained, was that everyone in the world should have a chance to be happy.

Early in the spring, a little before her death, something must have happened. She became withdrawn, preoccupied, and made long transatlantic telephone calls. Once she had burst out, exclaiming to Jessica, "It's so mixed up. When I started with this, I never thought—"

She had caught herself, and would not say more. She began avoiding people, which was not characteristic, and closing the door whenever she was in her room. Could she have had some premonition? Was someone stalking her?

That was ridiculous. Why would anyone? Certainly not at Hudson College, in pretty, pastoral Fort Sheffield.

But there had been that worry, and those phone calls and strange remarks . . . and Weyland. All unexplained.

Not that she owed Jessica any explanation; it was only what had happened in the end. Poor frightened Françoise.

19

3

In the morning, after a Continental breakfast of rolls, coffee, and a crisp croissant in the hotel dining room, Jessica went back to the pedestrian mall. It was damply fresh and warm in the morning sunshine, and scarcely less crowded than it had been the night before, despite the fact that it was Sunday and nearly all the stores were closed.

She had supposed they would be, but she could still look at them and see what there was. Window-shopping, she picked out for herself a yellow tee shirt with *Nice, Côte d'Azur* emblazoned in dark-blue flocking. There were bright dish towels printed with Provençal recipes, and costume dolls in regional dress. She found a newspaper store open and bought a copy of *L'Express,* so she could practice reading French.

She returned to her hotel room just as the phone began to ring.

"Am I speaking to Meess Hayden of Kennersville, New York?" inquired a male voice with a French accent, which she detected at once as phony.

"Steve, you'll have to do better than that if you want to disguise yourself. How was Marseilles? Are you still there?"

"No, I'm in Nice. Marseilles was hot. Nice is hot. And I don't want to disguise myself, I want lunch. Have you eaten yet?"

"No, I've been browsing around the stores."

"With all this sea and sunshine going to waste? Forget the stores, grab a nice little bikini, and meet me downstairs in half an hour."

She did as she was told, fortunately managing to cram her swim things into her capacious handbag, so the hotel would not know she had borrowed their towel.

Steve arrived, looking more relaxed than he had on the train, in navy-blue slacks and an open-neck shirt.

"Did you see your friends?" he asked.

"No, I just got in late last night." She did not mention that she had called them. She was still ashamed of her own ineptitude, not knowing where she was to meet them, or even fully convinced that they would keep the date.

He asked, nevertheless. "You didn't call them, or anything?"

"I couldn't get up my nerve." It was half true, at least. "After all, they never answered my letter."

"So you're not going to try to see them."

"I'll probably try. That's more or less why I allowed so much time in Nice."

They were walking along a narrow street toward the beach, past a travel agency and then a small café. His hand tightened on her arm. She thought it was a signal to stop at the café, but he kept walking.

"I think you should forget the whole thing," he said. "Why rake it up for them and for yourself?"

"I've already—" She bit back her words.

"Already what? You did call them?"

"I've already promised myself I'd do it. It was like a promise to Françoise. Are you asking me to be dishonorable?"

"I'm asking you to have some sense."

"Steve, we've been over this before. They know she's dead. It's not as if it would be a shock to them. If they don't want to see me, all they have to do is refuse."

His fingers loosened. "Well, I don't know. I guess

you're right. It's just that it seems so morbid, in a place like this, to be brooding over someone's death. I think you should spend the time with me instead."

"I am spending time with you, right now. Didn't you notice?"

He chuckled. "I see I'll have to keep working on you. In the meantime, peace again?"

"Peace."

By manipulating a series of push-button traffic lights, they crossed the busy boulevard and reached the promenade that ran along the beach.

There were two kinds of beaches, she discovered. There were those that were open to the public free of charge, where the bather was on his own, sitting or lying on the formidable stones that carpeted the shoreline. Then there were the privately managed beaches, for which one paid a small entrance fee and acquired the use of a dressing room, a comfortable mattress, and an umbrella. Steve led her down a flight of steps to one of the latter. They changed their clothes, rented a pair of mattresses, and left some possessions to hold their claim. Then they took a table on the terrace of the bathhouse and ordered lunch.

A substantial *salade Niçoise* and a glass of rosé wine. With the inevitable French bread, it was enough for her.

Steve asked, "Are you sure you won't starve?" She shook her head.

"Okay, then, you know best. Tell me, what did you study in college?"

She broke a slice of bread from the partial loaf in the basket. "I don't know how it happens, but we always seem to talk about me, never you."

"I'd rather talk about you. I know all about me."

"All right, since you ask, I got my degree in European history. Very practical, isn't it?"

"Practical for this trip, anyway," he said. "Where are you going after Nice?"

22

"Westward through southern France and then to Spain."

"And then?"

"Northern France."

"Not Morocco? That's the usual thing to do from Spain."

"It isn't usual for me. I'm not made of money."

"Doesn't cost much to pop over to Morocco. I should think you'd want to see something really exotic."

"I would, but a budget is a budget. Besides, my daddy'd panic at me wandering around the Casbah by myself."

"Afraid you'd get carried off by white slavers?" He shook his head. "Dear me, the notions we Americans have about some of these places. Didn't you know anybody from that part of the world while you were at college?"

"Not Morocco. Should I have?"

"I don't mean Morocco specifically. Here you are, consumed with curiosity about Europe. Why not the, uh—the Moslem world?"

"One thing at a time, for heaven's sake. After all, Europe is my field."

Their lunch arrived at that moment. Steve sat back and gazed at the ocean, then asked, "What do you plan to do with a degree in European history? What kind of job can you get?"

"Probably nothing. I'll be going to graduate school in the evenings, and I'll have to get some kind of job in the daytime. Then maybe try to teach, if I can. I understand a history degree is a drug on the market these days."

"Lotsa luck. You're pretty ambitious, aren't you?"

"I guess I am. It took my parents a while to understand that, and they're still not sure what it's all about, but now I think they're actually proud of me."

"You're an only child?"

"Yes. I imagine, more than anything else, they'd like to have grandchildren—" She blushed, feeling that she had gotten herself into some kind of trap. "But there's plenty of time for that."

They finished their lunch, then lay on the mattresses, and after a while went into the water to swim. She found that the stones, although smooth and rounded, hurt her feet. By watching how other people did it, she learned to wear her shoes down to the water's edge.

"I do like sand better," she remarked when they returned to their camp, "but these mattresses make it all worthwhile."

"Just be careful you don't get sunburned. We have a long evening ahead of us."

There it was. After his various lectures, she could scarcely admit that tonight she had a date with the Lanniers.

"I'll tell you," she said, "after a day in the sun I usually feel pretty zonked out, and I do have to wash my hair."

He looked at her over the top of his sunglasses. "Come now, Jessica, that's the oldest excuse in the book. There's nothing wrong with your hair."

"Nothing but a good dose of salt, and that's terrible for hair. It's not that I don't enjoy being with you, Steve, but I'm awfully tired and I'd like to get to bed. Alone."

"One little dinner won't make it too late."

"Yes, it will. In France, dinner can last for hours."

In spite of his argument, Steve was relatively graceful about the turndown. But as they walked back to her hotel an hour later, he said, "I'm going to call you during the evening and make sure you're washing your hair."

"If I'm in the shower," she replied, "I probably won't hear the phone. And if I do, I may not answer."

She bade him good-bye in the lobby and started upstairs. At the first landing, she looked back. He was still there. He waved to her. She waved back and went on up the stairs, but she felt disturbed. It was odd that he re-

24

mained there watching her, and that he was so adamant about her not seeing the Lanniers.

But then, she should not have lied about it. That was rather odd, too.

4

Later, as she stood before a mirror drying her hair, the telephone rang.

Steve, she thought. Checking up.

It was not Steve. It was the deep, accented voice she had heard on the phone last night. "Hello? Miss Hayden? This is Marius Lannier. I shall come for you in my car at seven-thirty. We will go to dinner with my mother and her friend. Is it all right?"

"It's perfect," she exclaimed, pleased that he had called, but not intending such effusiveness. "Yes, I'll be ready. The Hotel Foster." Although he knew that.

"I'll wait in the lobby," she added. "It's a small lobby. And I've seen a picture of you, so I think I'll know you."

"Very good. Seven-thirty." He hung up abruptly.

She finished drying her hair and searched for the perfect dress in which to meet the Lanniers. She had not brought many, and after trying them all, decided on a pale-blue knit that draped softly over her body. Its shade was subtle with her reddish hair. She completed the effect with a long string of fake pearls. Imagine, she thought, dining with the Lanniers in fake pearls.

At seven twenty-five she went to the lobby to wait. At seven-thirty, he came.

She knew him from the picture, although he was taller

than she had expected. Over six feet, probably. Unusual for a Frenchman.

It was like seeing the portrait come to life. There was the same fine, straight nose, the hair that really was dark, unlike his sister's, the sensuous mouth, which also managed to look stubborn and unapproachable. His somber expression, the same as in the photograph, was accentuated by the dark suit he wore.

She rose to meet him and introduced herself. Even then, his face did not change. She felt a wall go up around him, belying the gallantry with which he took her hand and gently touched his lips to her fingers.

"Yes, I am Marius," he assured her distantly. "So you recognized me. How could you know me?"

"I told you, Françoise had a picture of you. I saw it every day."

He acknowledged that with an indifferent nod. She had thought he would be pleased to know of Françoise's regard for him.

"Shall we go?" Lightly guiding her elbow, he led her out to his car. It was a gray Peugeot, which he had left double-parked near the hotel entrance. Already it was attracting the attention of a policeman. Marius spoke briefly to the officer and helped Jessica into the car.

As they drove off, he explained, "I was about to be punished for blocking the traffic. It is good that you were ready."

"I'm glad, too." She suppressed a comment on his use of the harsh word "punish." He would take it as a criticism of his English, which was certainly better than her French.

"Isn't your mother coming?" she asked.

"My mother was not ready when I left. I didn't want to keep you waiting, so we will go back."

"But you shouldn't have bothered. I could have taken a taxi."

"It is not out of the way. We are going to Villefranche."

27

She tried to puzzle that out. Perhaps his mother was not out of the way on the road to Villefranche, but Jessica definitely was. And yet she must learn to accept these attentions as her due. Françoise would have. Probably any Frenchwoman would.

"I love your city," she said. "This whole area's so beautiful. I haven't seen much, I just got here yesterday, but I went to the beach with a friend, and—"

"Do you know someone in Nice?"

"No, just an American I met on the train."

Marius stopped for a traffic light. Without bothering to look at her, he asked, "Why did you come to Nice?"

"Because—why not? It's Françoise's city and she was my friend. She talked about home, and her family. And besides, I'm a tourist, and that's what tourists do."

"She talked about us?" The light turned green.

"Yes, often. She told me—when she decided not to go home for the summer, she hoped I'd look you up. You see, she already knew I was planning this trip."

He concentrated on guiding the car through a crowded street and did not answer.

She asked, "Have you ever been to the United States, Mr. Lannier?" To herself, she thought of him as Marius, but did not know what degree of formality he would expect.

His jaw tightened. "Once. In April of this year. I went to bring back her body."

"Oh . . ." Then he was in Fort Sheffield. She wished she had known. "How long were you there?"

"For one day only."

She murmured, "It must have seemed too much, even so, under the circumstances."

The car began to climb into the hills that surround Nice, the foothills of the Maritime Alps. The houses on these streets were pleasant, of pastel stucco with red tile roofs and tropical gardens. She looked back and saw the

28

city spread below her. The next moment they turned a corner and she could see nothing but a banana tree in someone's back yard.

Higher and higher they climbed. Then the road leveled and began to wind its way toward Monaco and Italy. Rounding another bend, they stopped before a wrought-iron gate on the right-hand side of the road, where the mountain dipped toward the sea.

Marius got out of the car and opened the gate. He drove the car in, parked on a white gravel terrace, and went back to close the gate.

On that steep hillside, the house was mostly below them. Very little of it was visible, but from what she could see, it appeared more modest than she had expected. And yet it was beautiful, a small, exquisite jewel in a lovely setting of oleander bushes, agave plants, and masses of purple bougainvillea on the retaining wall, which was cut through by the steps they now descended.

The house itself was pale yellow stucco, an architectural enchantment of wrought-iron balconies and long windows that faced the sea. The garden in front, perched as it was on the steep hillside, was nothing but terraces and bright flowers. Below it lay almost the entire city of Nice, and beyond that the aquamarine waters of the Mediterranean.

"Oh, it's beautiful!" Jessica exclaimed. "How could Françoise bear to leave it?"

"I wish she had not," he replied, his face stony.

A maid opened the door for them, which seemed a rather unnecessary gesture, since Marius had had to manage the driveway gate by himself. The house was dim and cool, with all the long windows covered by green plastic blinds against the afternoon sunshine.

Almost at once they were joined by a petite, slender woman with delicate features and a magnificently cut black dress. Belatedly it occurred to Jessica why Marius wore a dark suit, even in the subtropical summertime. They were in mourning, of course.

Mme. Lannier, softly scented, embraced her and greeted her effusively. She seemed much warmer than her son, and for that Jessica was grateful. She was a young-looking woman with an unlined face that was subtly but thoroughly made up. Her platinum hair was exquisitely coiffed. She was of a completely different generation from the very natural, spontaneous, and blue-jeaned Françoise.

Marius addressed a question to his mother in French. She answered him briefly, then burst into English, including Jessica in the conversation with a wide gesture of her arm. "I am so angry," she exclaimed. "A friend of mine, Mr. Claude Augustín, he was supposed to go with us, but I talked to him on the telephone only a few minutes ago and he cannot come. He has suddenly a business conference. I can't believe it."

"Why not?" Marius asked. "It's your business that he takes care of."

"That's very true, but so suddenly? *I* knew of no conference. I don't understand it. But we will not talk of that. Perhaps he only rests, because he works so hard." Mme. Lannier turned to Jessica, bubbling, "It is very patient of you to come back here for me. I could not be ready in time, and Marius was angry with me. There were so many telephone calls, one after another."

Marius asked her mildly, "Is it necessary to answer the telephone every time?"

"Perhaps not—now." A cloud passed over the beautiful face. "When Françoise was away I always answered, until that one—call—"

Impulsively Jessica reached out to touch the woman's hand. A look passed between Marius and his mother, and Mme. Lannier managed to hide her sorrow, as though drawing a cloak around it, and become cheerful and gracious once more.

30

"A glass of wine before we leave," she said, "so we can learn to know each other a little bit." She led the way into the living room. It was comfortably furnished in cool blues and greens to counteract the Mediterranean heat.

"We will open one of the shades and let Zhessica see the view," she continued. "It is gloomy in here with everything closed, no?"

The view at first was blinding yellow sunshine, after the darkened interior of the house. In a few moments it sorted itself into the magnificient panorama Jessica had seen from the driveway, with the tall flowered spike of an agave framing one side of the window.

"You see, I, too, have lived in the United States," Mme. Lannier said, as she settled onto the couch. "Long ago, when the war came, my parents sent me there to study, so I would be safe. Probably nothing would happen to me here, but I was a young girl and they were afraid."

Marius looked up sharply. It seemed to Jessica that he was thinking of another young French girl who had not been safe in the United States.

"But I was glad," Mme. Lannier went on. "It is very interesting to see other places. Where else have you been, Zhessica?"

"Nowhere else," Jessica admitted as the small, dark maid passed around glasses of wine. "This is my first trip to another country in my whole life. I haven't even been to Canada. But I'm hoping to see a lot of Europe this summer. I have a return flight home from London near the end of August."

"It is good that you will have so much time," Mme. Lannier said. "And how long in Nice?"

"A week. Nice is special, because of Françoise. I won't stay that long in other places."

As no one responded, she went on, "I'm so glad I could meet both of you. I was afraid you might not be in town, or—"

31

"But we are nearly always in town," said her hostess, "and you were my daughter's friend. I am so happy that we can meet *you.*"

Marius did not look as happy as his mother did. He sipped his wine and stared briefly out of the window. His manner, although cool, was not actually rude. Jessica wondered if he resented his sister's having befriended her. He might have disliked Americans.

Or perhaps it was because she was of a different class than they, which in Europe seemed to matter more than in the United States. Her parents were shopkeepers, and she was the first member of her family ever to attend college. The Lanniers, on the other hand, were well established. Sophie Lannier, she knew, had brought to her marriage a flourishing perfume business that had been founded by her grandfather. Her husband, a manufacturer of cement and related products, had helped his wife with the perfume company and together they had made it grow. After his death there had been various directors, but she was still the president. Marius had little to do with that enterprise, but had taken over the management of the cement company.

All this Françoise had told her with some scorn. "My father, making *perfume,*" she had exclaimed. "It is not so bad for my mother. She's a silly woman anyway, with her jewelry and hairdressing appointments. But all they cared about was making the money. They could have been doing something important."

"I suppose they did what they knew how to do," Jessica had answered, "and it doesn't really hurt anybody, does it? Besides, the cement works is important. Or at least it's macho."

"You don't understand," was Françoise's reply, and Jessica had retreated, agreeing that she probably did not.

Mme. Lannier set down her empty glass. "Shall we go to dinner now?"

They went out to Marius's car. The older woman settled herself in the back seat, which left Jessica in front with Marius. "Now you can see better the view," Mme. Lannier told her.

They descended the hillside and drove along the Lower Corniche to the neighboring town of Villefranche. There they stopped at a restaurant, which, at first, could not be seen very well. Like the Lannier's house, it was below the level of the road. As with most such buildings, the initial view was only a modest back. The façade that looked out toward the sea was what mattered. They were led to a terrace overlooking the town and the harbor and seated at a table under a broad umbrella, which cut off the reddening evening sun.

Jessica allowed them to choose her menu for her. More wine was poured, and then began a leisurely procession, mainly of seafood dishes, all beautifully displayed. There was *soupe de poisson* with croutons, which were dipped in a spicy sauce. There was something chopped and served in clamshells with a mild garlic sauce and Provençal herbs, followed by *salade Niçoise,* and then a main dish of crispy fried fish.

"I hope you like fish," Marius said to her. "This is our specialty on the Côte d'Azur."

"I love it. And it's cooked so nicely here. At home, in my town, you can hardly get fresh fish."

They would probably think she lived in a desert.

Mme. Lannier said, "I am glad you were a friend to my daughter. It must have been a great help to her."

"It was good for both of us," Jessica replied. "I'm not sure I actually helped her much. Françoise was pretty independent."

"Too independent," Marius put in. "She should have known better than to go out alone so late at night."

"She was coming back from the library," Jessica said. "It was about nine-fifteen. I don't think she considered that late. And in Fort Sheffield, nobody ever thought... It just wasn't like that."

"Then you are wrong," he accused. "If it was not like that, she would still be alive. She should have known. A place where they all have the guns—"

"Marius, it's not true," Mme. Lannier exclaimed, embarrassed before their guest. "Not everyone has a gun."

"You're right, there is a lot of crime," Jessica said, "but really, so much of what you hear is just the way the newspapers blow it up. And anyway—" Françoise had been killed with a knife, but she would not bring that up. They already knew it.

"There is crime in Europe, too," Mme. Lannier said. "Too much, recently. It is bad everywhere."

Marius refilled Jessica's glass from the wine bottle on the table. "I'm sorry, I have not the right to talk that way. It's not your fault. It only makes me angry. You see, at the last minute she decided it would be fun to go to school there. So instead, what happens? She is killed."

"It makes me angry, too," Jessica said. "I feel terrible about it. That's one reason I wanted to see you people. I wanted to tell you how sorry I am."

At least she now understood some of the reasons for his chilly manner. It seemed that Steve might have been right after all.

Mme. Lannier burst out, "So terrible. It's as if something evil is coming into our lives. Only last summer, you know, a very good friend of the family, of my late husband, was killed. He was managing our perfume factory."

Marius said in French, "I don't think we should talk about that."

"Killed," she continued, paying no attention, "in the bath, in a cheap hotel."

Marius made a face, resigned, it seemed, to his parent's lack of discretion. In a cheap hotel—the implication was obvious.

"Martin." Mme. Lannier seemed almost to be talking to herself. "A very old friend of my husband. Bernard Martin. But, of course, it is worse with Françoise. My own daughter. This I cannot believe."

"Of course not," Jessica said. "I can't really believe it either."

Bernard Martin. Françoise had mentioned something about him, but for the life of her she could not remember what it was.

"Did she have other friends?" Mme. Lannier asked.

"Oh, yes, dozens. There was another girl who was quite close to her. Eileen Fowler. Her aunt and uncle owned a clothing store in town. That's where Françoise got her red jacket. We had a fair to raise money for the scholarship fund. Eileen borrowed some mannequins from the store and Françoise made French folk costumes for them. She was always doing things like that. Always giving parties. And she'd invite everybody, the faculty, the kitchen help ... "

Marius said, "Françoise was sometimes, how do you say? Undiscriminate?"

"Undiscriminating," Jessica corrected him gently. "Yes, she was, but I think it's a nice thing. She was never snobbish or bigoted. She just loved everybody."

"That is good," he agreed. "But this undiscriminatingness of hers ... It is not good to trust everyone. How can we know what happened?"

His mother winced.

"Oh, I don't think it was that," Jessica said. "The police checked out everybody very carefully. Everybody she knew. It would have to be a stranger, someone who didn't know her."

Unless it was Weyland.

After Françoise's death, she had broken her promise and told the police about him. It seemed vital then, but they had decided he could not be a factor. He had gone before she died. As far as Jessica was concerned, that would have

35

been the end of it, except for his sudden reappearance on her Nice-bound train. She wondered if he could possibly know she had mentioned him to the police.

"Do you know a man named Weyland?" she asked.

Marius set down his wine glass. "Who is that?"

"He's someone who visited Françoise, just a little before—well, in April."

She had meant to avoid speaking of Françoise's death, but was probably calling more attention to it this way.

She went on, "Françoise didn't want me to talk about him. But when I was coming here, I saw him in the train station in Paris. He saw me, and looked horrified. Then he went in a different direction, but when I arrived in Nice, he got off the same train as I did. I wondered if he was a friend of hers from here."

"Perhaps." Marius shrugged. "I didn't know all her friends."

His mother exclaimed, "But how strange that you should see him, too, in Paris."

"Not so strange," said Marius. "Many people take the train from Paris. What did you say is his name?"

"Weyland. That's all I know. Just Weyland. I don't know if it's a first or last name."

"I never heard of anybody named Weyland. He went to visit her, you say, in the United States? But you think he is not American."

"No, only I'm not sure he's French, either. I don't know what he is."

"He was there when she died?"

"No, about a week before. And then he left."

Marius looked thoughtful. Jessica was sorry that she had brought up their tragedy again. She made a pretense of studying the view, determined to change the subject.

"It's so fascinating here, the way the mountains come right down to the ocean. On that train trip from Paris, of course, all the countryside was beautiful, but at Marseilles you get these amazing rock formations, and after that it goes along the coast. It's just gorgeous."

"Yes, it is an interesting trip," Mme. Lannier agreed, "but very long. I always think Americans are in a hurry. Was it better than the airplane?"

"Much better. The plane costs too much, I couldn't even consider it, and with the train, I saw everything along the way."

Mme. Lannier chatted about the different parts of France and what there was to see. The meal continued at a leisurely pace while the sun set and lights went on in the harbor. The Corniche, curving around the bay, became a string of diamonds in the soft evening haze.

Finally the last demitasse was drained and they rose to leave.

"This has been just lovely," Jessica said, and repeated, "I'm so glad I could meet you."

"It was entirely our pleasure," Mme. Lannier assured her. "I hope we will see you again before you leave Nice."

They drove her back to her hotel, and Marius saw her to the elevator while his mother waited in the car. Jessica thanked him once again and offered her hand. He pressed it gently, met her eyes for a moment, then let her go and stood back, as though the moment had been an accident.

The elevator arrived, and reluctantly she stepped inside. He raised his hand in a brief salute. A very faint smile touched his mouth. As the door closed, he turned and walked quickly away.

She felt unaccountably empty as she rode to the third floor. It should not have been the end, after a pleasant evening spent together. That was how she had originally imagined it, but now she did not want them to pass so quickly out of her life.

She unlocked her room, switched on the light, and started toward the window to open the heavy shutters and relieve the stuffiness.

Halfway to the window, she stopped. Something about the room bothered her. She could not tell what it was. There was no disorder.

She flung open the bathroom door and turned on the light. She opened the doors to the wardrobe. She looked under her bed.

Silly. There was not even a smell of someone there. Or perhaps it was all subliminal, something that registered only on her unconscious mind, for this had happened to her once before.

She looked again in the wardrobe. The clothes were draped haphazardly on their hangers, and she was sure she had hung them neatly, so they would not become wrinkled.

She opened her suitcase, on its rack next to the wardrobe. There she found the disorder. All her lingerie, which had been carefully rolled, was tossed about at random. Her shoes had been removed from the plastic bags in which she kept them. Her cosmetic case had been opened and the contents scattered.

Her head felt dizzy and her throat dry. If anything, this was worse than being accosted on the street. Her room, her sanctuary, had been violated. She was not safe anywhere. It was an echo, almost exactly, of a similar occurrence at college. And it had happened not long after Françoise's death.

Of course the maids had access to her room, but this was not the work of a maid. They tidied things, and even if they stole, they would do it neatly, subtly, since the first suspicion would fall on them.

All this raced through her mind as she reached for the telephone and called the desk.

"Monsieur?" she said when the night clerk answered. "Someone's been in my room. All my clothes are messed around. Can you send somebody?"

"There is nobody here," the clerk replied, then seemed

to think better of it. "I will try to find someone. You have something stolen?"

"I don't know yet. I'm still checking. But please? *Tout de suite?*"

"*Immédiatement, mademoiselle.*"

Ten minutes later she answered a knock at her door. It was a man whom she recognized as the daytime concierge. How he must have hated being bothered. Perhaps, at that, ten minutes was *immédiatement.*

"I don't think they stole anything," she explained, having taken an inventory while she waited, "but I don't like this at all, somebody coming into my room and throwing my things around."

"Did you have your door locked?" he asked.

"Of course, and I had the shutters fastened. No one could have gotten in without a key, but somehow I don't think it was a hotel employee. It's too messy, too ruthless. You see?" She opened the wardrobe and showed him her disarrayed clothing, at the same time realizing that he could not know what it had looked like before. Swallowing her modesty, she unlatched the suitcase and showed him her lingerie and shoes, explaining how she had left them.

"Perhaps the maid?" he suggested. "Sometimes they unpack for you."

"It *was* all unpacked. And any maid, trying to be helpful, would hardly leave such a mess. No, monsieur, someone got into the room. Maybe they were looking for something, but of course I had nothing valuable. Maybe they went into some of the other rooms?" she asked hopefully, afraid of the implication of being singled out. But he denied that there had been trouble in any other room.

"It's the security I'm worried about," she said. "Someone getting in. What if I had been here? Maybe I should call the police."

"Oh, no, no, mam'selle, there is no need to call the
39

police. We will handle everything. But I assure you, there is nothing to worry about. No one can enter here."

"But somebody *did*."

"Mmm." He was clearly skeptical, or at least unruffled. "But as nothing was stolen . . ."

"I don't like people coming into my room and messing with my things."

"I can assure you, mam'selle, there is no way anybody can get in. You see, you can go to sleep now without any fears. We are watching over you."

"You don't believe me, do you? Probably you think I left it this way myself."

"It is possible, perhaps. Looking for some beautiful dress to wear to dinner with the young man."

So they had even seen the young man. And she had spent considerable time trying to find the right thing to wear. But what she could not get through to him was the fact that she would never leave her own clothes in such a tangle. If nothing else, they would get wrinkled, and she had no travel iron.

The concierge left her feeling a little less on edge, but certainly more annoyed. How dare he call her a liar? She was tempted to change hotels, but that might be difficult at the height of the tourist season, and it would scarcely make a ripple at the Foster. They would simply rent the room to someone else.

The only thing to do was to discuss it with Steve. She called his hotel and fortunately found him in.

"Someone's been in my room, ransacking my stuff," she told him.

"Good God, while you were washing your hair?"

"No," she sighed, bored with stories, "I did go out. I had dinner with the Lanniers. That's the family I told you about."

"You what?"

"It's like this, Steve. You were acting so possessive, I

didn't want to discuss it with you. I'm sorry. But now I'm calling you as a friend. Someone ransacked my room and the hotel won't take me seriously, since nothing got stolen. What should I do?"

There was a silence so long that she wondered if he were still on the line. Then he said cheerfully, "Move in with me."

"No. Something practical. No games. It really bothers me that someone's been here. And I don't like being treated like a harebrained idiot who might have done it herself."

"Sweetheart, I don't know what to suggest, except that you may have trouble finding another room at this time of night. We'll talk about it tomorrow, okay?"

He wished her sweet dreams, and hung up. She turned out the light and sat for a long time in a chair by the window, gazing out at the leaf shadows in the alleyway.

The intruder had not taken anything, so what did he want? If he was searching for valuables, it was hardly logical that he should try only her room. Or even pick this rather modest hotel to begin with.

And it had happened at college, too. But there couldn't be any connection.

Or could there?

Her thoughts kept going back to Weyland. She did not know why, except for Françoise's secrecy about him, and Françoise's death, and now his travels, which seemed to parallel her own.

A coincidence? Perhaps.

Or maybe Steve was right, although he had said it differently, and she ought to get going on the rest of her trip.

Even Steve . . . he had seemed so terribly anxious to keep her away from the Lanniers.

Or maybe the Lanniers themselves . . .

She blockaded the window with her suitcase and then studied the directions for the travel alarm clock her father

41

had given her. It had a chain attached to it, the end of which slipped into the door to act as a burglar alarm. She had been more amused than anything else when her father explained how it worked. Poor old Dad, always worrying about his daughter, especially in far-off lands that he himself had never seen or understood.

With the chain in place, she began to feel safer. As though Dad himself were there, watching over her.

5

She woke to a loud ringing. Fumbling frantically, she tried to shut off the alarm, but the ringing went on.

It was a bright daylight and she could see the door clearly. Nothing appeared to be disturbing it. Then she realized that the ringing was the telephone.

She picked it up, to be greeted by Steve's hearty voice.

"I understand you want to get out of that room. How'd you like to go on to Italy today? Sorry it can't be Rome, but I'll give you a ride as far as Genoa."

"Not today," she told him sleepily. "I've hardly had a glimpse of France yet. And I don't really care to go to Genoa."

"Home of Christopher Columbus."

"It's not on my list. I'm still doing Nice, but thanks, anyway."

"I only meant Genoa as a starting point. I should think you'd want to get away from this town. Can I see you before I leave?"

"Okay, but you'll have to wait. I'm not even dressed."

"All the better." She could almost feel him leering over the wire. "You slept well enough for a girl who was terrified last night."

She agreed to meet him in an hour. It was odd, but she really had slept well, although "terrified" seemed a bit exaggerated. It was more a case of surprise and apprehension, but now, in the daytime, even that seemed ground-less. She realized that it would not have been anything personal. It was only a maid, searching for jewelry. Or, more likely, for some extra cash, which would not immediately be missed because it had not been counted. Poor maid. Wouldn't most people have more sense than to leave money around a hotel room?

By the time she met Steve in the lobby, the hotel dining room had stopped serving breakfast. They went out to look for a snack bar where she could have coffee and perhaps a sandwich.

"That's what you get for sleeping so late," he teased her. "You must have had a wild evening with those Lanniers. Too bad I haven't time for the beach. It would be nice and restful for you."

"I don't think I could take another day at the beach," she said as he steered her into a tiny café. "And the wild part came later, after I got back to my room. At least it was wild on my nerves." She wondered how he knew the name Lannier. She must have mentioned it to him.

"Who all was there?" he asked.

"In my room? How should I know? But it was all so *déjà vu,* because—"

"No, dear, at dinner."

She had to shift her mental gears. "Just the Lanniers, Mama and big brother Marius. And me."

"That's all?"

"They took me out. It wasn't a party or anything. Why do you want to know?"

"Just curious about how you spent your evening." He picked up a lock of her hair and let it fall. It was a moment before she recalled the significance of that allusion.

"You must have noticed it's cleaner," she said. "I really did wash it, as soon as I got back from the beach." She studied the menu briefly and ordered cheese omelet and coffee.

"For once I'm getting away without a Continental breakfast."

"And that in itself is an achievement," Steve said. "What did you talk about with the Lanniers?"

"Mostly about Françoise. What else? And we talked about the scenery in France and my train trip from Paris."

"What did you say about Françoise?"

"What is there to say? I told them how she'd been at school. We talked a little about how she died."

"Yes? What about it?"

"Really, Steve, what is this inquisition?"

"Not an inquisition. Only my natural curiosity. She was a friend of yours, wasn't she? In fact, it was because of her that you were on that train where I met you. I'm interested, that's all."

She hoped he was not going to be sentimental about the train trip.

"Mostly," she said, trying to answer his question, "her brother thinks the United States is a savage place and she never should have gone there. And I told him nobody ever believed a thing like that could happen in Fort Sheffield."

"And, since it did, it shows he's right. It is a savage place. And didn't I tell you they might resent your intrusion? You should have stayed away from them. Listen to Uncle Steve sometimes."

"They didn't resent *me*. At least the mother didn't. She was lovely. And the brother was ready to resent anyone and everyone. But he was lovely, too."

She did not know what had made her say it. Fortunately, their coffee arrived at that moment and distracted him. But she thought again of Marius, his anger about his sister's death, which he had taken out on Jessica, and at the same time, his Continental gallantry. She could still feel that last touch of his hand.

"So you fell for the guy," said Steve.

"I wouldn't say that. He wasn't very nice."

"Lovely, but not nice."

"Well, yes. That just about sums it up."

The waiter brought her omelet, golden and dripping with cheese. That, and the usual basket of bread, would make it the heartiest breakfast she had eaten since landing in Europe.

Steve said, "I hope you have something to remember your friend by."

"Why do I need anything? I have my memories."

"Oh, you know. Some sort of keepsake."

"She wasn't the sort of person who was attached to things. She even opposed her family's money and all that sort of materialism. In a way, she was really kind of radical."

"Radical how? Revolutionary?" He watched her intently while he absentmindedly tore a chunk of bread into tiny pieces.

"No, I don't think so. Maybe not radical, but socialistic, or utopian. She wanted everybody to be happy, and thought if the money were spread around, then people who were desperately poor could at least have a chance."

He grinned. "Kind of a simplistic philosophy, don't you think?"

"Yes, but refreshing. When you get into the more sophisticated versions of it, such as Marxism, it turns psychopathic."

"Now what do you mean by that?"

"Have you ever read the *Communist Manifesto*?" she asked.

"Properly known, I believe, as the *Manifesto of the Communist Party*."

"Okay, okay. Anyhow, it's positively paranoid. All that stuff about the bourgeoisie causing everything from typhoons to the Black Plague. It's—paranoid."

Steve sat laughing to himself and crumbling another piece of bread.

"Actually, I haven't read it," he said. "But I didn't bring you here to discuss politics. Just to say good-bye, for now. What are you going to do with yourself when I'm not around to keep you busy?"

"I'm going to do what I started out to do. See Europe. First Nice, then I'll head on into Provence."

"Where are you going in Provence?"

"All over. I want to see Avignon, Arles, Nîmes, Les Baux. I'd love to see La Camargue."

"Les Baux is very touristy," he said.

"Oh, well, I still want to see it. And what will you be doing? Does this count as work, this trip to Genoa?"

"I'll be in Italy for a while." He brushed off her question. "Are you going to see more of Françoise's family?"

"Not that I know of. I think it was hello and good-bye."

He studied her for a moment, probably still thinking she had fallen in love with Marius, and wondering if she was to be satisfied with hello and good-bye. Then he looked at his watch and signaled for the check.

"Another appointment?" she asked as they left the restaurant.

"Still plenty of time."

She had thought he would take her back to the hotel. Instead he started toward the beach.

"Where are we going?" she wanted to know. "You told me you didn't have time for the beach."

"I just thought we'd walk by there for old time's sake." Gently he rested his hand on her elbow.

She looked around suddenly, hearing footsteps. "Hang onto your wallet. There are a couple of creeps back there."

He turned, at the same time patting his hip pocket to be sure the wallet was still there.

"You shouldn't do that," Jessica warned. "Now they'll know where you keep it."

He laughed. "It seems we can both give advice on foiling crooks. You were the one who didn't know enough not to advertise your home address when you're traveling."

The two men behind them crossed the street and vanished down a narrow lane.

"Glad they're gone," she said. "This street isn't very busy, is it? They could hold us up and nobody'd know."

He answered with a chuckle. "Never fear, Steve is here. And, for all you know, their intentions could have been perfectly innocent."

They reached the boulevard, crossed it, and began to walk along the promenade overlooking the beach. The day was bright, with a warm breeze blowing in from the sea.

Africa, she thought. Africa's right over there. The Sahara Desert. That's where this breeze is coming from.

She leaned on the railing and looked out at the lazy water. "Does the Mediterranean ever get turbulent?"

"Of course it does. There have been shipwrecks all through history. Don't you remember your Homer? And a couple of years ago this whole beach area was devastated by a wave."

He stood back and she thought he seemed impatient. If he felt that way, she wondered why he had brought her here.

"Actually, Steve, I really don't feel much like walking now. I'd rather save my feet for sightseeing this afternoon. If you want to talk some more, maybe we could go and have another cup of coffee."

"Just like an American," he grumbled. "Another cup of coffee. Don't you want to walk up to the next block and go back that way for a change of scene?"

"Oh, all right." She strolled along beside the rail, dragging her hand on it. He moved away, apparently expecting her to drift with him. But just in front of her was a display of sidewalk art. She hugged the rail to avoid stepping on a portrait of Napoleon Bonaparte in colored chalk.

"That's really good," she said. "I wish I'd brought my camera. Do you mind if I go and get it?"

He was shocked. "Why did you leave it in your room, especially after somebody's been ransacking the place?"

"It's only a cheap Instamatic. And they didn't take it last night."

She turned to go back the way they had come. Steve looked exasperated. His attitude disturbed her. She had, after all, come to Europe by herself, and she almost preferred it that way, having the freedom to do as she pleased without being accountable to anyone.

"I'm sorry," she told him. "I'm just not going to miss a shot of this Napoleon. It'll be something to show the people back home."

"Anything you say." He was making an obvious effort to be pleasant, but it was also clear that she had somehow gone against his wishes.

During the afternoon she toured the Cimiez section of Nice, visiting the old Roman baths, the arena, the Archeological Museum, the Matisse Museum.

She spent a pleasant evening alone, eating dinner early in a modest café, walking the length of the pedestrian mall, and then visiting the Promenade des Anglais to see the beachfront by night.

She woke in the morning, refreshed and happy. The last vestige of jet lag had gone. Or perhaps it was anxiety that had gone. She had taken care of the Lanniers, put the searched room behind her, and was ready to begin the rest of her holiday.

By the time she had dressed and eaten breakfast, it was nearly nine-thirty. The stores would be opening soon. She took the precaution, as she had the day before, of locking her suitcase and bolting the shutters. Slinging her handbag over her shoulder, she went down the stairs and through the lobby.

Outside on the shadowed street, Nice was rushing to work. Cars and motorcycles buzzed past her in the freshness of an early day. It was another of the soft, mild mornings that seemed a part of this city, and she looked forward to the chance to wander by herself.

At the first intersection, she emerged from the shade into moist, clean warmth. Sunlight slanted down onto her face and into her eyes. She started across the street.

Suddenly, out of nowhere, a motorcycle roared straight toward her. She staggered backward and lost her balance. Before she could fall, a pair of arms caught her.

"So early," a voice purred in her ear, "and in such a hurry?"

She fought to see, but the sun was in her eyes. A blurry glimpse of wavy hair, a wide head . . .

She caught her breath. "What do you want?"

Weyland turned her so that she faced him, keeping a grip on her arm. "Is that the way to greet an old friend? Come and sit in my car and we will talk."

"Talk about what?" She tried to pull away. His grip tightened. Like a noose, she thought wildly. The kind that pulls tighter the more you struggle.

"Just to say hello." His voice was smooth and soft, creamy velvet. He led her to a small black car parked a little way down the street. She looked about, thinking to scream, but no one would hear her. The seemingly lifeless buildings presented solid walls and shuttered windows.

He guided her firmly into the car. She might have resisted, jabbed her elbow into his stomach, but he had muscles of steel. Now it was too late. He climbed in beside her and started the engine. The car began to move.

She tugged at the door handle. It would not open.

He said, "I do not recommend to exit the car in traffic. You saw how even a motorcycle comes very fast. They can do serious damage."

She glared at him. "Did you set up that motorcycle?"

"Set it up?" he asked innocently. "I was simply on my way to see you."

"Oh, really. Would you please tell me why? And why you had to kidnap me?" She searched the door for a lock that she could open. To her dismay, there did not seem to be one. She tried the handle again.

He laughed softly. With a nod, he indicated the door

51

and her struggles. "What is this? You know me as the friend of your friend, is that not true?"

"I don't know if you're a friend. I don't know if you were even *her* friend." She gave up on the door and let her hands rest in her lap.

"If you wanted to speak to me," she went on, "you've had plenty of chances. There was the Gare de Lyon, and I know you were on my train that day. I saw you get off at Nice."

"Always you are with the young man. I do not want to interfere. Also, I do not know this young man. I may wish to avoid him, yes?"

"That's up to you. And I wasn't with him in the station. Either station."

"Oh, but many other people are there."

She sank back in her seat, feeling a strange loss of will. There was nothing she could do.

"Where are you taking me?"

"Only for a little ride, to renew our too short acquaintance."

"I wouldn't say it's too short. It's not short enough. You must have some reason for doing this."

"I have a reason, but what is your hurry? Always the big rush. I suppose, being American, you want me to get to the point."

"Even more than that, I'd love it if you'd just let me go."

"No doubt that you would," he said, "but it is out of the question. There is too much—what do you say? It is a gambling term. Too much at stake."

"Maybe for you there is, but I don't know anything about your problems, and I don't want to know."

"You don't want, but you are already involved."

"In *what*?" She turned angrily to face him. He only laughed and clicked his tongue.

"Tsk, so you say, but how do you make me believe

52

you? The more you argue this, the more I am suspicious."

My God, she thought. "But—what? Involved in what?"

"You ask me that already," he told her sharply. "I conclude that you must be involved, because there is no one else. But you are acting so strangely, I begin to wonder *how* you are involved."

She opened her mouth, but did not speak. She was hardly the one who was acting strangely, but this had ceased to be a matter for repartee.

He said, "Tell me first, if you will be so obliging, did anyone else come to see Françoise? Anyone from France, or someone who was not with the university?"

"I guess so. Actually, it's only a college, not a university. Once I saw her having dinner in town with two men, and they were speaking French."

He pounced on her answer. "When was that?"

"Back in the winter, sometime. Maybe February."

"I am talking about later. When she was killed. I asked if anyone came to visit her."

Did that mean he hadn't killed her?

Or only that he wanted to find out how much they knew about him?

She busied herself with the zipper on her purse, afraid that her face or her voice might betray her. He would know she had gone to the police. She wondered if he could be extradited.

"Please," he said. "This is important."

Undoubtedly it was. "I already told you," she replied, "I don't know. If somebody was there, no one in Fort Sheffield knew about it. The police checked very carefully."

They were winding through crooked streets, in an area she did not recognize. The window on her side was closed. She could feel the heat of the sun beating through the glass.

She could also feel him watching her. She glanced at

53

him to see whether he was paying attention to his driving. He was, but watching her at the same time.

"And Françoise," he said. "Did she give you anything in those last days? Anything to bring with you here? That is what I really want to know."

Steve had asked her the same question. Why? Why so much interest? It was only a picture. And Françoise had meant it as a keepsake. Not to bring here.

But she had. Jessica felt her face go pale as she remembered Françoise's sentimental request.

She looked at him from under her lashes. He did not appear to have noticed her sudden reaction.

In those last days, Françoise had given her the picture. He had accused her of being involved in something. The picture must have been part of it.

"No," she said, carefully glazing her face as she stared ahead at the street. If he knew she had the picture, he would never believe in her innocent ignorance.

"Did anybody come to her room then, after she died?"

"Oh, yes. The police."

Startled, he asked, "Why the police?"

"Because Françoise was murdered. They always do that. It's part of the investigation."

"There was nobody else?"

"I honestly don't know. They locked the room to keep people out. And they took everything away. They probably gave it all to her brother when he came."

"They took everything that was hers? Everything?"

She closed her eyes. "All I know is, after it quieted down, there was nothing left in her room. Just a mattress on bedsprings, an empty dresser . . ."

"That is not what I want to know."

"It would help if you'd tell me what you do want to know." She straightened abruptly. "Weyland, are you the one who searched my room?"

He turned to her with a quick frown. "Searched your room? When is that?"

"Sunday night somebody broke into my room and went through my stuff. Since it's obvious that I'm not Sophia Loren traveling with a fortune in jewels, I'd just like to know what they were looking for. And the same thing happened at college, only a few days after Françoise was killed."

It was not a coincidence, or a maid looking for cash. It was the picture. Or something else to do with Françoise.

He said, "You were not there when this happened?"

"Of course not. I was having dinner with Françoise's family."

A sharp intake of breath. "You have seen them? Françoise's family?"

"That's what I said."

He stopped for a traffic light. Once more, stealthily, she tried the door handle. It moved, but did not open the door.

He mumbled in French, "This is bad."

Guiltily she pulled away her hand.

"I am talking to myself," he said. "I did not know you could understand French."

"Almost none." She gathered that he was distressed at her having seen the Lanniers.

"When will you leave Nice?" he asked.

"Next Sunday. Why?"

"I am only wondering. It would be better if you leave sooner. Why do you want to stay?"

"Because it's Françoise's city. I came because of Françoise."

Sudden interest. "Because of her? What do you mean?"

"I just wanted to see it, and meet her family. She wanted that. I made all my plans before she died."

"And you talked to her of this trip. But she gave you nothing before you came?"

"Why should she give me anything?"

It's the picture, she thought again. *But why? It's only Françoise and—and—*

"It is what I expected," he said. "Maybe I am wrong. But maybe not. Why don't you leave Nice very soon? It would be better for you."

"Better for me in what way?"

"I do not have to tell you that. You must take my word. I only ask you to remember what happened to Françoise. Now go back to your hotel room, pack the bags, and get on a train. I don't care where you go."

"Good God," she said angrily. "Do you really think you can kick me out of this city? You don't own the place, as far as I know. I've had my vacation planned for four months, and I don't intend to let anybody ruin it."

"It might be more ruined than you expect," he told her calmly, "if you will not follow my advice. I must also warn you not to speak of this meeting to anyone. Not to anyone. Now here is your hotel. Adieu, my dear young lady. That means 'to God.' It is my wish for you."

They had rounded a corner and there, miraculously, was the Hotel Foster. He reached under the dashboard. She heard a click, and now the door opened when she pulled on the handle. She looked at him for a moment, scarcely believing that it was over and he was letting her go. He nodded good-bye. She slid from the car and walked quickly into the hotel.

7

Back in her room, she sat in the big chair next to the window and tried to think. Only one thing began to make sense, and that was Françoise's death. It made sense because it was no longer a random robbery, or so he had implied.

But everything else, which she had thought was simply her own life, her trip, her dinner with the Lanniers, was total confusion.

He's crazy, she decided, but it gave her small comfort, for she knew it wasn't true. Something was going on. He was involved in it, Françoise had been, and he supposed that Jessica was, too, one way or another.

And it was something that must be kept from the Lanniers.

Oh, hell, she thought, and opened the notebook in which she had listed all her hotels, with their addresses, telephone numbers, and dates. She put through a call to the one in Marseilles, in which she had a reservation for Sunday night.

Could they make that tonight? Was anything available right away?

No, mademoiselle, they were very sorry, but nothing was available. The hotel was completely booked for many weeks. Did she want them to hold her room for Sunday?

"Yes, I guess so." And then, fearing they might misunderstand such vagueness, she added, "Yes, please do."

She hung up and stared at the clock for a while before she saw it. Ten-thirty. If she was checking out of the Foster, she would have to do it in the next half hour, or pay for another night. She would not have time to go to the travel agency down the street, book another hotel in Marseilles, come back and check out of the Foster, all before eleven. She did not want to give up her present room until she found another, and could not afford to pay for two.

Can I afford to be killed? she wondered.

If only Steve were here. He would inject a note of normality into all this. Probably he would scoff at Weyland and tell her it was all part of her Agatha Christie complex.

He had not left any address, yet Genoa was not so far away. Why hadn't he left an address? A phone number?

On a chance, she called his hotel, but he really had checked out. They could give her no more information than that.

She was alone. The only people she knew in all this city were the Lanniers. They were not really friends. Would they even understand if she tried to tell them what Weyland had said about Françoise? *I ask you to remember what happened to Françoise.*

She reached for the telephone, then stopped. Weyland had said she must have nothing to do with them, or tell anyone about his visit. Had he said that? She could not remember the exact words. But they had a right to know about Françoise, and the picture.

Marius would be at work now, but his mother might be home. She was the more sympathetic one, and spoke better English. Jessica picked up the telephone and put through her call. Too late it occurred to her that all this might be something Mme. Lannier would not want to know about her daughter.

Too late, she wondered if her call might be intercepted. Weyland had known where she was staying, and a hotel

58

switchboard scarcely guaranteed privacy.

The phone was picked up almost immediately and her ears assaulted by an agitated babble. The voice did not speak English or even very coherent French. Twice she caught the word "gendarmes." Then she heard a male voice in the background, and Marius came onto the phone. He spoke in French.

She answered in English. "This is Jessica Hayden. Is something wrong?"

There was a quick exhalation as he switched languages and mood.

"We had a little excitement last night," he told her offhandedly. "A burglar, it seems. It is nothing." He was clearly reluctant to let her, an outsider, know that he had been ruffled in any way.

"I'm awfully sorry to bother you." She really was. For a moment, his trouble seemed worse than her own.

"It might not be just a burglary," she went on, feeling her way.

"What do you mean?"

"Something happened to me just now. That's why I'm calling. It's about your sister."

"My—You say something happened to you? Wait a minute, maybe it is better not to talk on the telephone. Can I see you sometime? Where are you?"

He understood better than she had thought he would. Perhaps he suspected something after all.

"At my hotel," she said.

"You are alone?"

"Yes, of course."

He asked for her room number. She heard him repeat it. Then he said, "I cannot leave now, the police are here. Maybe in an hour I will come. You will be there?"

"Yes, I'll be here."

She paced the room, then sat in the chair again and felt the midday heat coming through the window. Something began to prickle her, a feeling. She wondered if Weyland could be out there, watching. Or maybe there were others. She wished she had known what he was talking about. She moved away from the window, then went back and closed the shutters.

It was less than an hour, but it seemed much longer before she heard a knock at the door and his voice speaking softly. "Zhessica, are you there?"

She opened the door. He came quickly into the room.

"I have not much time," he said, and noted the closed shutters, which already made the room still and stifling. "Are you frightened of something?"

"I just thought . . . it seemed better, that's all."

"Maybe it is." He went over to the window, pushed open the shutter, and looked out.

"I think you are safe," he said with a little smile, but she noticed that he carefully latched it again. "Tell me, what is the problem?"

"Well—you know that man I told you about, who visited Françoise? The one I saw on the train?"

"Yes."

"This morning he—he grabbed me on the street and forced me into his car."

She looked for an expression of shocked surprise, but Marius only waited politely for her to continue. Was none of this news to him? Had he expected something like it?

"Does this sort of thing happen all the time in Nice?" she asked sarcastically.

"No more than anywhere else, I suppose," he replied. "Maybe less than some places. But I think it is not the fault of Nice that it happened to you. There are other things, and I want to know about them. I want to know all you can tell me. Do you have some time now? Perhaps you can come with me. I must go to my mother's factory, something has happened there, too. The best place to talk is in the car."

Dazed, she collected her handbag and room key.

"What do you mean 'other things'?" she asked. "What other things?"

He motioned her to be quiet as they stepped out into the hall. She double-locked the door and tried to make inconspicuous small talk as they went down the stairs.

His car was parked around the corner, this time legally. She looked about for Weyland. If he was there, watching her, of course he would be hidden. She must not worry about it. He was only one man. But still she felt relieved when they started on their way.

"Now tell me what you were talking about," she said as they pulled away from the curb.

"I cannot tell you much, because I don't know much," was his answer. "It is only that I have been wondering about Françoise, about some of the things she was doing and the people she knew. And now, what you tell me, I am thinking that maybe this has something to do with why she died."

"That's what I thought," said Jessica. "That's why I called you. I thought you should know, but it seems you're ahead of me."

"Not very far ahead, since I know nothing. And I did not before think it had to do with her death, because she died so far away."

"I wouldn't have thought so either, except for Weyland," she said. "What happened at your house? Was anything stolen?"

"I don't think so. It was that someone came in and turned some things a little bit upside down. But only in my bedroom, and the room that was Françoise's."

"That happened to me, too. While I was out with you on Sunday night, someone searched my room. I called the concierge, but he didn't believe me. Was it in the evening? Were you out somewhere?"

"No, it was later. During the night. I—was not there."

61

He seemed reluctant to mention that fact. He must have spent the night with a girl friend, she concluded, probably gone home in the morning to shower and change, and found his mother in hysterics.

He said, "Now tell me what happened to you. This man took you in his car? The man who knew Françoise? And how did you escape?"

"I didn't have to. He let me go." She described her encounter with Weyland, the things he had wanted to know, and what he had said to her. Marius was silent, frowning at the road as he drove.

"Weyland," she repeated. "That's what he calls himself. For all I know, he lives here in Nice."

"He is French?"

"It's hard to say. I met him in Françoise's room and they were speaking French. I think I took them by surprise. They seemed a little disconcerted. And later Françoise asked me never to tell anyone he was there."

She watched the streets and houses rush past, and remembered her ride with Weyland.

"If this man warned you not to have anything to do with us," Marius said, "why do you call me?"

"I told you, I couldn't let it go like that. It has something to do with your sister, and I thought you had a right to know. And now look, they've involved you, too. Someone broke into your house and searched Françoise's room. But I didn't know you were already alerted."

"Not for this. I did not think they would do anything to us. Now someone, too, has been making trouble at our factory. So you have told me everything you can think of?"

"Yes, everything." Again she looked out of the window. They were leaving the city behind them.

"How far away is the factory?" she asked.

He stared at her briefly in surprise, but it turned out to be surprise at himself. "I am sorry. It is in the mountains, near Grasse. A few kilometers. Do you have enough time?"

"Oh, yes. All day."

A mountain hideaway, she thought, suddenly, for a moment, fearful of Marius, too. Yet Grasse's reputation as a perfume center was a fact.

"How come it's so far from your home?"

He smiled faintly. "My father, you see, had his own business, and the office is in Nice. Now I work there myself, in Nice. My mother keeps a small house in Grasse, and sometimes she stays there, to be near to her factory."

"That gets complicated, doesn't it?"

"Yes, it does. But I am sorry," he said again. "This is a long way to go. I was not thinking."

"That's all right. It's fun to sightsee."

"It's too bad we cannot see more, but I must hurry. Already I am late because we have the trouble at home, too. My mother, she is very upset to see that they have been in the room of Françoise. It brings everything back. She feels sick, so I must go myself."

"Your poor mother. She's such a lovely person. It must be terrible for her."

She thought of her own parents at the airport. How terrible for them, too, if anything should happen to her.

"I wonder," she went on, "if he really did. I mean Weyland. If he did kill Françoise, he'd kill anybody. Not that I'd mind for myself, as long as it's quick and doesn't hurt, but my parents—" To her horror, the jumbled words built into a sob. All the strain of the day broke forth, and she began to cry.

The car swerved. "Zhessica!" He slammed on the brake. It slowed the car but did not stop it as he leaned toward her, his hand on her arm.

She held her breath until the wheel was under control, then murmured, "That was stupid of me."

"No, it was stupid of me." He had regained his composure, and seemed to forget all about the moment of compassion he had shown.

After a while he said, "This man you tell me of. The police must not think that he is the killer, no? If they say it was a robbery."

"Well, what happened was, he'd already left by the time she died. He'd been gone a week. And it really looked like a robbery. They took her purse and wristwatch."

He frowned, as though in pain. She thought: How odd that personal possessions can be so much a part of the person.

"And I believed it," she went on. "I never imagined— not till I saw him at Gare de Lyon, and the way he looked at me. As if he was horrified to see me. If he didn't have anything to hide, he would have just said hello, because obviously he remembered me. I thought he got on another train, but then I saw him again at Nice. And I still might not be sure, except for this morning. But it's strange, I couldn't really tell whether he was saying he did or didn't kill her."

"So he followed you to Nice?"

"I don't really think so. He looked too surprised when he saw me. It must have been an accident. As I said, maybe he lives in Nice. Maybe he knew Françoise, but why—"

"What does he look like?"

They were out in the country now, heading into the mountains. He drove very fast, but handled the car with great skill.

"I'm not very good at describing people," she said. "He's not as tall as you are, maybe five eight or nine. That's feet and inches, I don't know it in meters. And he has wide shoulders. He looks powerful. And a wide head."

"Yes? Go on."

"His hair is very wavy. Dark, with a little gray. His eyes are dark and deep set. His face—even his face is muscular. It's not smooth or soft. I'd say—well, he might be about the same age you are, but he looks older."

There was a long silence. She began to think he had not paid attention. Finally he said, "You are not sure of the name."

"I didn't think Weyland was a French name."

"That is his only name? It is Weyland?" He pronounced it delightfully. She tried not to smile.

"It's the only name I know."

He gestured toward a small zippered wristbag that lay on the seat between them. She had noticed that nearly all young Frenchmen carried such bags. They preferred it to cramming their possessions into various pockets, especially in the tight jeans and sports pants that many of them wore.

"In there you will find some pictures," he said. "Try to see if you can discover the man you are telling me about."

Cautiously she opened the bag and found a plastic folder of snapshots. "In here?"

"Only to see. What you tell me, I think he looks like someone I know."

She leafed through the photographs, stopping at one of a young woman, airy, bright, and suntanned, in earrings and lipstick, and bearing a strong resemblance to Françoise.

"Who's this?" She held up the picture.

He asked in amazement, "You don't know?"

"Is it Françoise?"

"Yes," he answered with a sigh, "it is Françoise. I thought you knew her very well. But it is true that she changed from the time that picture was taken." He nodded toward the photograph in her hand. "This is how I like to remember her."

"This is how I would have expected her to look," Jessica said, "after I met you and your mother and saw the way you lived, but she wasn't like that at all. She was, I don't know, more down to earth. No makeup, jewelry, or

65

fancy clothes. She was a lot of fun, but she was serious, too. And her hair was different."

"Yes," he agreed quietly, "that is what happened in the last year. Everything changed. It was from the inside. How she felt about things. She used to fight with us very much."

"I think, if she'd looked like this when I knew her, I'd have been afraid of her."

"Afraid? Why?"

"Intimidated. She looks so elegant and self-assured. All the things that intimidate me about other women, especially European women."

"But why should you feel intimidated?" he wanted to know.

She wondered why she had mentioned it in the first place. "It puts me at a disadvantage, doesn't it?"

"But why? To be elegant and self-assured is not everything. Other things are important, too."

She looked at him in surprise, wondering exactly what he meant, but he was concentrating on the winding mountain road.

From the folder in her hand, a second young woman smiled up at her, as elegant, as poised as Françoise, and even more beautiful. Jessica stared for a moment, then quickly flipped to the next one.

"There!" In a picture with another man. "The one on the left, with a tennis racket. Is that who you thought it might be?"

Marius glanced at the folder and nodded.

"His name is not Weyland, it is Henri Harger. Yes, I know him, and so did Françoise. I cannot believe—No, Henri would not harm her."

Jessica thought it over. "If it's the same man, and he wouldn't have hurt her, then why did he threaten me this morning? He had something, some skeleton in his closet."

Marius leaned politely toward her. "Some what did you say?"

It was an untactful choice of expression, and she did not try to translate it.

"As if he was hiding something. He wanted to get me away from Nice. He definitely didn't want me to see you, and I can't think of any reason, except that you might somehow find out that he'd visited Françoise. And why would he try to hide that, unless—?"

"Maybe it had nothing to do with the death of Françoise."

"But it did. He said so."

Marius was thoughtful. Finally he admitted, "This is very confusing to me, to speak of Henri in this way. He is a very—I don't know how to say it. A very intelligent person. Very practical."

"Level-headed?"

"Maybe that is what I mean. Do you understand? I think you do."

"I understand what you're saying, but—well, maybe I have the wrong man. He kept talking about Françoise. Of her death. And then he warned me away."

"We will ask him what he means."

"But he said if I told anyone—"

"Henri will not hurt you."

"I hope you're right. He was very serious about it."

"So? We will find out what is the problem. Maybe Henri is in some kind of trouble, and we can help. He does not live exactly in Nice, but in Vence. It is not far. We can go there on the way home. You will like the mountains."

"I love mountains."

Especially when they led straight to the wolf's lair.

"If it really is your friend Henri," she said, "do you know what surprises me about him? He doesn't have a French accent."

"No?" Marius seemed amused. "Do you mean he speaks English like an American?"

67

"I don't mean that at all. He definitely has an accent, but it doesn't sound French. Not like yours, or Françoise's."

"That is interesting. Maybe that he spent so much time in Arabia. The place where he comes from, I don't know how you say it in English."

"He's Arabian?"

"Only half. His father came from Aden. That is on the south part of Arabia. First it was protected by Great Britain, and now is a separate country."

"Yemen. That's Yemen, or one of them, anyway. Does he really come from there?"

"As I said, only half. His mother was French. He lived in Aden when he was young, then he came with his mother to France and took her name."

"I thought his name sounded French, even if he doesn't. But he speaks French fluently, and even English very well."

"He is, as I said, a very intelligent person. That is why I am confused. He is too intelligent to do anything foolish."

"Oh, no, nobody's that," she replied. "Anybody can get carried away, or boxed in, or whatever makes people do foolish things."

He shook his head. "I can imagine it of Françoise, but not Henri. Françoise was very emotional. She would often be carried away. But the thing she was doing—and I still don't know what it was—I never thought it was so serious that she could die from it. Also, I did not know it would reach all the way to the United States. Now I must find out what it is. That is why I wanted to see you. Maybe together we can find some answers."

"And maybe that's why your friend Henri didn't want us to get together. Did you ever think of that?"

"Yes," he answered wearily, "I have thought of very many things. But I still do not believe Henri—maybe he went there to warn her. Maybe he knows something. That is what I want to ask him."

Again she said, "I hope you're right."

As they climbed higher into the pre-Alps, Marius told her
something about where they were going. Grasse and other
towns like it, he said, had developed in the mountains because, until the last century, it was dangerous for small
settlements to exist along the Mediterranean coast. They
would be constant prey for the Barbary pirates. Commu-
nities either had to be inland, or very heavily fortified.

"That's interesting," she responded, but her mind was
elsewhere. "Marius, if it was your friend who grabbed me
this morning, why do you think he's been using a different
name? That bothers me. There's something peculiar
about this whole thing."

"We will ask him, if we can find him. They told me he
has not come to his laboratory for several days."

"His laboratory? What do you mean?"

"He works in a laboratory at my mother's factory. He
is a chemist, a very talented chemist, but he likes to work
alone, so we give him a special laboratory. He is working
on such things as to stop the perfume from getting stale.
You know, something they can add to keep it longer without destroying the fragrance. Things like that."

"Was it his laboratory that somebody broke into?"

"His and one of the big ones. When they called us on
the telephone this morning, they said he has not been
there for a while."

"Well, I don't know. I hope it's all right just to go and confront him."

Marius chuckled as he changed gears for a steep hill. "Of course it's all right. What will happen? All he can do is refuse to see us if he is not in the mood."

"This morning he wasn't kidding around." Although, admittedly, Marius knew him better than she did. "Why would he choose the name Weyland? It's not even French."

"Many names are not French. Marius is not French."

"What is it, then? It sounds French."

"That is the way we say it. But it is Latin. A Roman name, from the Roman general Marius, who had his army at the place of the waters, which is now called Aix-en-Provence. That was before the Christian times. There were barbarian tribes, very savage, who came from Germany and attacked Provence. They were killing everybody and ruining the country, but Marius defeated them and saved our people. So even today it is sometimes a custom in Provence to name someone Marius."

She remembered having seen something about it in the Michelin guidebook.

"Do you mean the Provençal people still admire Marius?" she asked. " He wasn't really a very nice person."

"Do you know about Marius?"

"Oh, not much. But my field at college was European history."

"Really? You are a scholar?"

"Well, I wouldn't say that. But you have to study something at college, and I think history is fascinating."

"So do I, in fact. And to answer your question: as I said, Marius saved the people from the barbarians. There would be no Provence if he did not do that. As for the other things he did . . ." And the modern Marius concluded his remarks with a Gallic shrug.

The car wound farther into the mountains. Over a

sweep of ridges and vales, she could see small villages nestled among the hills. A warm haze hung in the air, adding to the feeling of sticky heat. Despite it, the air felt dry and the sun shone with uninhibited and perhaps unnecessary generosity on the browned landscape.

Marius nodded toward the mountain straight in front and above them.

"Do you see? There is Grasse. Now we take this little road to the factory."

He whipped around a corner onto a narrow lane, past a vineyard and a stone farmhouse on the left. The road zigzagged up the hill. They passed another stone house on the right, and then suddenly they were in the midst of cool trees. Marius drew up to a pale stucco wall and parked. Painted on the wall, in huge black script letters, was the name *Parfums Broucard*. Two tour buses stood against another wall of the L-shaped building, under the welcome shade trees, which some forebear had been thoughtful enough to plant.

"Do you give tours of your factory?" she asked.

"Yes, of course. We invite the groups, and we have people to guide them in different languages. It is a good way to advertise and to sell the perfume. There is one bus, you see, from the Nederland, and one from France. After the tour we take them to our shop, and they can buy some of the great perfumes. We manufacture many, and they can buy them here more cheaply because we sell them with our own label."

"Do you mean the really famous perfumes? Shalimar, and things like that?"

"No, not Shalimar. The Fragonard factory makes that and many others, but we have some, too. We are only a small family business, not big, like Fragonard."

He ushered her into the building through an inconspicuous side door. They entered a corridor with offices on either side. Marius paused in the doorway of one of the

71

largest. Its stocky, gray-haired occupant was talking on the telephone. Finishing the conversation, he looked up and saw them.

The man's face remained without expression, while Marius grinned broadly.

"Zhessica, I would like you to meet Mr. Claude Augustín, who is the most important person in this establishment. He is the manager for our president. Claude, I want you to see what you missed when you did not have dinner with us on Sunday night. Miss Zhessica 'Ayden, from the United States. She was a friend of Françoise."

Mr. Augustín bowed and smiled, but did not make any move to circumnavigate his massive desk or even lean across it to shake her hand.

"It is my pleasure, Miss Hayden. I am so sorry I could not dine with you the other night. I had a business meeting."

"It's nice to meet you, too," Jessica said.

"I have just learned," Marius went on, "that Zhessica is a scholar of the European history."

She protested, "Marius, really, you're dignifying me a little too much."

"But why not? I like the intelligent women, and I think Claude does, too. He was very fond of Françoise."

"Ah, yes, my poor little Françoise," Monsieur Augustín said sadly. "You had better go to the laboratory, Marius. The police are waiting for you."

Something had been nagging at Jessica, and still did as they left the office.

"How funny," she whispered to Marius. "He reminds me of someone, but I can't think who."

"Maybe he is like someone you know. Or maybe he, too, went to visit Françoise at the university? He does travel sometimes."

"No, it wasn't that. I don't think I've actually met *him* before, but there's something about him that reminds me of someone, only I don't know who."

72

Her confusion was interrupted by two pretty young women in green lab coats who rushed up to Marius, each grabbing an arm and chattering rapidly in French.

Flanked by the two girls, he made his way down the corridor. Jessica trailed after him, feeling forgotten. They went through a pair of heavy wooden doors, through a lobby or reception room, then another pair of doors, and another, into a large, bright laboratory. Two policemen were there and the conversation was loud and lively. Jessica waited by the entrance, wondering if she even ought to have come in.

With the gendarmes accompanying him and gesticulating, Marius began a tour of the laboratory. The work-tables and chemistry apparatus had not been disturbed, but along the walls drawers had been pulled out, papers scattered, and cabinets emptied. When they reached the row of windows on the outside wall, one of the policemen pointed to a jagged hole in the glass. Only a small hole, but large enough to put an arm through. The windows were hung on top-mounted hinges and could be opened from the bottom with a crank. The burglar, or whoever it had been, had reached in, cranked open the window, and admitted himself. Even then, he must have been as slender and agile as a monkey to squeeze through the opening.

"And the other laboratory?" Marius asked.

A crowd had collected in the doorway. Suddenly it shuffled aside, and a striking figure sailed through and into the room.

It took Jessica only a moment to recognize her as the young woman whose photograph Marius kept in his wallet. The one who was not Françoise. The stunning, smashing-ly elegant young woman. From her picture, Jessica had gotten some of the full effect, but the reality was even more eye catching, for with it came a personality that seemed to command attention.

Her hair was blond, carefully shaded in gradations of silver and gold, and curled just at her shoulders. The color must have been artificially achieved, for the eyes were sooty black and, although the result was harmonious, it did not seem exactly natural.

She wore a white dress, pencil thin, with a cinched waist that set off an exquisite figure, and a lightweight jacket of hot pink. The jacket was certainly superfluous in view of the weather that day, but perhaps was necessary to complete the ensemble, the rest of which consisted of a white miniature poodle with a collar and leash of the same hot pink.

The girl paused near the doorway and, as though no one else were there, called a greeting to Marius.

He looked up from one of the cabinets, his hands full of papers. "Ah, Simone," he said abstractedly.

Simone wandered toward him, weaving among the lab tables, apparently determined to wrest his attention from the matter at hand. The rather emphatic dialogue was lost on Jessica. She regretted not having practiced her French more intensively. As a tourist, she managed all right, asking her way to museums and ordering dinner, but when they began shouting and waving their hands, she was lost.

Not that this exchange, however publicly performed, was any of her business. She edged back toward the doorway and tried to blend into the huddle of employees who had come to hear what was said about the break-in, but were melting away, uninterested in what appeared to be developing as a lovers' quarrel.

With a final remark, and what seemed a gesture of dismissal, Marius turned from the luscious Simone, and led the gendarmes through a door at the back of the room and up a flight of stairs. Simone murmured something to her dog, and on tiny heels clicked back out through the door.

Jessica followed, to wait in the corridor for Marius. She felt as superfluous as Simone's pink jacket, but could not think how to get back to Nice without Marius and his car.

The factory bustled around her, the chemists began to clean up their laboratory now that the police had seen it, and after a long, dreary, and awkward interval, Marius returned.

The gendarmes were still with him. He was busy talking to them and did not look at Jessica, but gently took her elbow and led her down the corridor to the lobby and main entrance.

There Simone stood waiting for them, with a glowing smile for Marius. The police left, and Marius introduced the two women.

He spoke in English. "Zhessica, this is my friend Simone . . ." The last name was a jumble of French syllables. "And Zhessica 'Ayden, from the United States. She was a friend of Françoise."

As though on cue, Simone's face became clouded. "Ah, yes, poor Françoise. Marius, I still cry about it." Then to Jessica, "And you, darling, how long will you stay in Nice?"

"Till Sunday," Jessica answered, and watched the sooty eyes light up.

"Only Sunday? Maybe we shall see each other again." Simone turned to Marius and began a conversation in *intime* French tones, her fingers sliding gently down his arm. On one of them she wore a large pearl ring.

Embarrassed, Jessica backed away and nearly tripped over the dog, which sat watching her with eyes as black as its mistress's. She reached down and scratched its head. It wagged its stumpy poodle tail, but did not attempt to stand up.

Marius caught the hand that rested on his arm, murmured something about having to go to Vence, and *"mon ami,"* and raised the delicate knuckles to his lips.

The hand was withdrawn rather sharply, a murderous glance directed at Jessica, and another argument ensued.

75

Marius was gentle but firm. Simone worked at the ring on her finger. Jessica thought she might be going to take it off and throw it at him, but it seemed that playing with it was her way of releasing tension. She dropped the dog's leash and he began to wander. It provided a welcome distraction for Jessica, who could occupy herself with retrieving and petting the animal.

Finally they seemed to reach an agreement. Simone, flashing a mechanical smile at Jessica, took the dog from her, whirled back to kiss Marius on the cheek, and walked down a short flight of steps to the front door.

"She's very beautiful," Jessica said.

"Perhaps," he muttered. His tact was exquisite.

"Does she live around here?"

"No, she lives in Nice. She came here because she heard that there was trouble. Would you like to see the factory for a minute before we go?"

"I'd love to."

At one side of the lobby a woman in a green lab coat was addressing a tour group in German.

"You have seen our laboratories," Marius said, gesturing toward the now-closed doors in back of the group. "That is where our chemists work. They are so sensitive that they can smell a perfume and tell you every one of the hundred and twenty essences that are in it."

"I don't see how that's possible."

"But you must understand," he explained as they climbed a flight of stairs, "besides being a doctor of the chemistry, they have to have a special talent, an excellent nose, and they are very experienced in these things. Now in this room—" He opened another heavy door. "Here is where we cook the flowers and extract the essences."

"Where do you get the flowers?" she asked. "Do you grow your own?"

"No, but the flowers are a very big industry here. There are many perfume factories and many flower farms in this area. You will see some of the farms on our way to Vence."

They wandered among mazes of boiling vats and distilling tubes and finally reached the room where the perfume was bottled. Young men and women in the inevitable green coats sat at long tables, gently easing the golden liquid into tiny glass containers. The room floated in a sweetness of mingled fragrances.

"I should think it would be quicker to bottle it by machine," Jessica remarked.

"It works better this way, by hand," he told her. "There is not so much room for mistakes. As you can see, the bottles are very small."

The workers seemed a cheerful group, most of them in their teens or very early twenties, chatting comfortably and joking with each other. Perhaps they moved on to more skilled jobs when they were older. Françoise, she remembered, had said they were not paid very high wages. Françoise had seemed to resent the entire operation, which had helped to raise her in luxury from the time she was born.

"What are you thinking about?" Marius asked as they left the room.

"About—Françoise."

"And so, once more it is Françoise. I, too, find that many things remind me of her. Would you like now to see our store?"

The store was also on the second floor, just above the lobby. Samples of perfume, soap, and bubble bath were arranged on long counters so that customers could sniff the fragrances. A tour group was there now. About forty people, she estimated.

"You must make a lot of money from these groups."

"Enough," he answered, "to pay for giving the tours. It does cost money. We have to have special people who can speak many languages."

"Then what's the point, if you just break even?"

"For public relations. Is it not a good idea?" He spoke to one of the women behind the counter, who reached to a shelf in back and handed him a small, gold bottle.

With a slight bow, he presented it to Jessica. "Here is our own special fragrance. It is called 'Mademoiselle Sophie,' after my mother. That is the name my grandfather gave to it, when she was only a girl. You will find it can last a long time in this gold-painted bottle, where it does not get the light."

"Oh, thank you!" Jessica removed the lid from the bottle, only to find an inner seal. The woman leaped from behind the counter.

"Here is one already open, mademoiselle. You keep the new bottle until you are home." She dabbed a drop from the open bottle onto Jessica's throat and more drops inside her elbows. A light floral fragrance with sensuous undertones filled the air around her.

"It's lovely! I never knew much about perfume—" They would guess that, for she had not worn any. "But I'll start using it from today."

The saleswoman, overcome with generosity, presented her with a larger bottle of the same fragrance in eau de cologne. "For after the bath."

Jessica thanked them both again, silently regretting that there would be no one around to smell it after the bath.

"And now," Marius announced, "we go to Vence."

They had been touring the factory for almost twenty minutes. In that time, they discovered when they reached the parking lot, Simone's small white sports car had not moved. Simone stood dejectedly resting against it.

"It won't start," she said to Marius.

Marius got into the driver's seat and was immediately sprung upon by the dog, who welcomed him joyfully. He turned the key. Nothing happened. He tried it twice more, then opened the hood, checked the battery, and

78

tried again. Jessica heard him ask how come the car ran well enough to get Simone all the way from Nice, and now would not start at all. Simone only answered with a shrug.

And then, when at his invitation they all began walking toward Marius's car, Jessica wondered if perhaps Simone knew more about engines than she was letting on.

It was an uncharitable thought, and probably a bit wild. How could anyone so impractical looking, with an immaculate white dress and long, lacquered fingernails, have successfully, and undetected, disabled an engine?

And yet it did seem a remarkable coincidence that the car could not leave just when Marius happened to be leaving.

Simone very generously allowed Jessica the front seat next to Marius, and climbed into the back with her dog. "So you can see better," she explained, as Mme. Lannier had done. "I have seen it all before."

Marius gave her a charming smile, clearly approving of her thoughtfulness.

They began a fantastic ride, looping through mountains on steep, winding roads. Marius pointed out a flower farm, where terraces of lavender bloomed on the mountainside. Around another bend there were terraces of roses.

He showed her perched villages, built on mountaintops as protection against the marauders of centuries past. Made entirely of indigenous stone, they looked almost a natural part of the mountain, and she was surprised to learn that they were still inhabited.

They crossed a dizzying gorge cut by the Loup River as it tumbled from the pre-Alps toward the Mediterranean. At one point the road was so narrow and kinked that cars would not have been able to slither past each other. A traffic light had been installed, seemingly in the middle of nowhere, to permit travel in only one direction at a time. After that, they drove through woods, with silver-leafed olive trees bordering the roadside.

"It's just beautiful," Jessica exclaimed. "I'm glad we came this way."

"I think I would have brought you here anyway, even if not for Henri," said Marius.

As they neared Vence, she could see hothouse farms for growing flowers, but with the mention of Henri, her apprehension had come back.

"Marius, I'm not sure this is really such a good idea."

"You have identified a man," he told her, "who was my friend for a very long time. I insist to find out what is happening with him."

That, Jessica realized, put much of the responsibility on her. But she could not be wrong in her identification. Weyland, or Henri, had a distinctive appearance, and he had known Françoise.

"He did warn me," she said again.

Marius inclined his head very slightly to remind her that Simone was sitting in the back, and hearing all they said. Jessica wondered what they were going to do about her when they actually saw Henri.

They drove down a shady street and stopped in front of a tall yellow house with neat white trim. Marius disappeared inside, and she waited in the car with Simone. The French girl murmured endearments to her dog, while Jessica studied their surroundings. This couldn't be where he lived, this quiet, gracious town house. It made the whole thing seem so improbable.

A few minutes later Marius returned, and indicated with a wide shrug of his arms that their trip had been in vain.

"Either Henri is not at home," he said, opening the car door, "or he does not want to see me. He has a front apartment, so he could know that I am here. Did you happen to see anyone at the window, on the very top?"

"I didn't happen to think of looking," she apologized.

"I didn't happen to think of suggesting it." He got in beside her. "We make a poor pair of spies, you and I."

Simone leaned forward. "Spies? What are you talking about?"

"We are spying on Henri," Marius said calmly. "He borrowed some money, and lost it at the casino."

Simone pouted. "Marius, it is not like you to fight with your friends about money."

"I have become hard," he told her, "in my old age."

Simone settled back, idly stroking the dog's head. "Let's go home now. Don't wait for Henri. I'm bored." She had lapsed into French, but spoke slowly enough, with a kind of plaintive drawl, so that Jessica understood.

"Not to cause any trouble, but just out of curiosity," Jessica said, "isn't Vence where the Matisse Chapel is?"

Marius looked at his watch. "The Matisse Chapel? Yes, do you want to see it?"

"Oh, no, it was only a question. I know you both have things to do."

"I will go to my office later anyway, but we can see the chapel if you want to. It's open now and it's very small. It will only take a minute."

She glanced uneasily at Simone, who said nothing, but gazed glassily into space.

"I really would like to, if Simone doesn't mind. I saw the Matisse Museum in Nice, and I got interested."

"Simone does not mind," Marius assured her, and repeated, "It won't take long."

Simone removed her pink jacket and sat fanning herself with a handkerchief.

The chapel was on a quiet street, and like so many buildings in that hilly area, below the level of the road, so that all they could see at first was a roof of white and blue tiles in a ripple design reminiscent of the sea. Rising from it was a tall, wrought-iron cross.

"Are you coming in?" Marius asked Simone. She shook her head and settled back more firmly in her seat.

The entrance to the chapel was down a flight of stairs,

at the foot of which sat a nun in a white habit, who nodded to them and murmured a greeting. To her left was the chapel, cool, white, and new, like a whitewashed cell in the blazing Mediterranean heat.

There was no red. That was probably what kept it cool. The stained-glass windows, with the sun shining through them, were jewels of blue, green, and yellow.

As they climbed back up the stairs to the street, Marius asked how she had liked it.

"It's fascinating," Jessica said. "It gives you a completely different feeling from the old cathedrals. So light and airy, and—clean. Not that the cathedrals aren't clean," she hastened to add.

"Probably they are not," he agreed matter-of-factly. "They are many hundreds of years old, getting dirty all the time. This one was built in nineteen-fifty."

"I think it's more the uncluttered, white effect," she tried to explain. He had ceased to listen. His attention was claimed by Simone, who had gotten out of the car to walk her dog. She moved slowly toward them with an easy, undulating grace.

Reaching Marius, she slid her arm through his, and with their noses only five inches apart, enveloped him in an intimate smile that closed off the rest of the world.

9

As she entered her hotel, the fragrant peace of Grasse and
Vence disappeared. She could think only of Weyland. She
glanced around the lobby, at the faces lounging in chairs or
standing by the desk, half expecting to see him waiting for
her.

To avoid trapping herself in the elevator, she climbed
the stairs to her room, and surveyed it quickly before she
closed the door. Unfastening the shutters, she let in an
afternoon breeze and the smell of musty old wood on the
window frame.

The telephone rang.

She stood still, wondering if he had seen her with
Marius.

It rang again. Better to answer it than not.

Steve's voice demanded, "Where have you been? I've
been trying all day to reach you."

"Steve! Where are you? Did you come back?"

"No, I'm still in Italy. And where were you?"

"I went to Grasse," she replied. "And Vence."

His voice sharpened. "What the hell were you doing
there?"

"Sightseeing. Have you ever been in those mountains?
It's the most thrilling ride I ever took."

"I'll bet. What do you mean by running around like
that? I tried three times to get hold of you, and all I got

was your hotel switchboard, so I'll be charged for it anyway."

She was too outraged to laugh. "I'm sorry for that, but I hope you don't think I came all the way to Europe just to sit around a hotel room waiting for the phone to ring."

"Of course not." He chuckled, but it sounded forced, or maybe she only imagined it. "What did you do, take a bus tour?"

"No, I went with a friend. I had to call about—something. As a matter of fact, I tried to get you first, just on the chance you might still be here, but you weren't."

"No," he agreed, "I wasn't. Who'd you go with? Who do you know around there except me? Not Lannier."

"Well—yes. I hadn't thought I'd see them again, but I had to call about something—"

"About what?"

She was silent for a moment, letting the question echo. What was wrong with him?

"Steve, I honestly do feel that my life is my own. I see no reason why I have to explain everything to you, or account to you for my actions."

"No, you don't, dearie. It's just that you're such an innocent, and this is your first trip abroad. Somebody's got to care what happens to you."

"I really doubt that anything's going to happen to me, at least from that quarter. Monsieur Lannier is as polite as they come, except for one lapse that first night when he wanted to blame me for all the violence in the U.S., and anyway he already has a girl friend who's ten times more gorgeous than I could ever be."

She was suddenly suspicious, remembering what he had just said. "Did my parents hire you to look after me?"

He laughed. "No, darling, I assigned myself the job, all unauthorized. So tell me about your trip. What did you do in Grasse?"

"I visited the Lanniers' perfume factory. What else would I do?"

"I just wondered. Was it educational? Did you get a guided tour?"

"Yes, I got a guided tour, I got a bottle of perfume, and I suppose it was educational. Anyway, it was interesting."

"Glad you had a good time," he said, "and that you find those Frenchies so hospitable. But watch yourself."

"Is that why you called, Steve? Just to check up? I thought, if you've been trying all day, it must be something terribly important."

"Don't you think you're important? No, really, I just wanted to find out how you're doing. Here I left you all by yourself, and I wanted to be sure you were okay. So take it easy, be good, and we'll have a nice dinner together when I get back."

"I didn't know you were coming back," she said.

"In a couple of days. Now promise me, stay away from all Frenchmen."

"In *France*? Steve, I really think—" He had hung up. "Damn," she said, and dropped the telephone onto its cradle.

She washed her face, removing the hot dust of the mountain roads. The sun was still high. Dared she go out to eat?

But in all these crowds. . . . She would simply keep her wits about her. This morning she had not been watchful, never expecting trouble.

She considered trying another restaurant, perhaps the seafood place on the next block. But her pizza café would be quicker, and she wanted to get back to her room before dark.

It was still early, and the café was not yet crowded. She placed her order and, while she waited, studied the guidebook she had brought with her. It seemed an innocent pastime, in case anyone should happen to be observing her, and would help to take her mind off Weyland.

After Provence there was Carcassonne, that medieval walled city where, at various times, Saracens and Cathari had barricaded themselves against attackers. Then the Pyrenees, and a side trip into Spain. Back to France, the magnificent châteaux of the Loire Valley. Brittany, Normandy. Then on to the Low Countries, and Germany. A cruise down the Rhine. Postcards every day to share the trip with her parents and friends. Not that her parents cared about Europe, particularly, they only wanted to know that she was safe and having a good time.

Safe . . .

She finished her dinner, such as it was, bought her day's supply of postcards, and went back to her room to write them and to fill in her diary.

The diary was for herself, to help her remember the trip in coming years. She debated whether to include the episode with Weyland. He was not a part of the trip that she cared to remember, but she doubted that she would forget him.

There was another thing. What if her room was searched again, and her diary found? What if he knew she had put it all in writing? She left it out.

Much later, when the sun had gone down, she climbed into bed to study her guidebooks once more. Tired from the hot, strained day, she soon turned off the lamp and lay dreaming with her eyes open.

A light from the alleyway shone through the tree outside her window, casting leaf shadows on the wall. A breeze stirred them, and as they moved, the shapes changed, grew larger at first, and then smaller.

Had the intruder climbed through the window to get in? He couldn't have, the shutters had been latched from the inside. He must have come through the door, must have had a key. The door was double locked now, but if he had a key, that would not stop him.

A motorcycle buzzed in the distance. Somewhere in another room, a couple argued in French. It would be fun to travel as a couple, in spite of the arguments.

She closed her eyes, thinking of the men she knew at home. There had been Al Higham, in Kennersville. He hadn't been able to think of anything to do with himself except join the army and become a paratrooper. He was stationed in Germany now, near Frankfurt. Everyone at home expected her to stop by and see him. She had not otherwise planned to visit Frankfurt, but it might be fun to see Al.

There was Nick Morrissey, one of her close friends at college. Nick's idea of a vacation was camping and fishing. He would not have liked Nice at all. He'd have made straight for Arles or Avignon and cast his line into the Rhône.

Her eyes closed. For a moment she felt herself riding in a car over the mountains, and then fell asleep.

She woke suddenly, her heart beating fast. It had been a loud noise, something close by. She did not even know where she was.

It came again, a pounding on the door. She opened her mouth to call out. No sound emerged.

She huddled in bed. They might not know she was there. Might go away. A drunk, trying to get into the wrong room. Beside her, the travel clock ticked, its chain neatly coiled on the night table. She had fallen asleep without remembering to insert it in the door.

The doorknob rattled violently. All she would have to do was call "Who is it?" and they would know they had the wrong room.

The rattling ceased and the furious pounding began again. It would wake the whole hotel. She picked up her phone to call the switchboard. There was no answer. A busy time of night, it seemed.

She lay besieged, waiting for someone to answer the

phone. It began to feel sinister, no longer a befuddled drunk. It was Weyland, battering her nerves.

Finally the pounding stopped and silence echoed in her brain. Only then did she become aware of a voice on the telephone. A tiny voice, squawking a question.

She spoke softly into the receiver. "There was someone at my door. It's stopped now. Someone pounding at my door."

"*Comment*?" asked the voice.

It was arrogant of her to expect them all to speak English, just because she could not cope with their language.

"Someone at my door," she repeated slowly. "Never mind, it's over now. Thank you."

She could not explain to the operator. It had stopped, but she dared not open the door to see if the person had gone. Gradually her reason returned. Anyone who truly meant her harm would scarcely have been so noisy about it. Someone had made a silly mistake, that was all. Perhaps it was the angry husband who had argued with his wife.

Cautiously she crawled out of bed, listened at the door, and then, as quietly as she could, slipped the end of her burglar alarm into the crack.

But the window . . .

The shutters would not close unless the casement window was also closed, and then she would suffocate. She placed an obstacle course of wastebasket, chair, luggage rack, and upturned suitcase by the window. For extra measure, she hauled the large easy chair over to the door and braced it tightly. And then she lay in bed and waited uneasily to fall asleep.

When she woke in the morning, she realized that she had indeed slept, but could not imagine how. The memory of the night came back to her. It did not seem so frightening with the sun shining outside, but she knew she could not go through it again.

It could happen anywhere, she thought. To anybody. A drunk, or a mixed-up, angry person . . .

But there *had* been Weyland. He must have known where she was staying. Her room *had* been searched.

Again she thought of leaving Nice early. But that would mean long-distance phone calls trying to book a room. Not knowing her way around, she scarcely dared arrive in a city at the height of the tourist season without a reservation. It would be so much easier to stick to her schedule and have her week in Nice. She hadn't even seen the flower market yet.

After breakfast, she set out to look for another hotel. She tried two small, inexpensive ones along the pedestrian mall, feeling that their very anonymity might be a good thing, but they had no rooms available.

She started back along the Avenue de Verdun, where a large concentration of hotels faced the sea. Time was growing short. If she did not have a new room by eleven, she would have to stay at the Foster.

After inquiring at desks and being answered by a series of shrugs and headshakings, she finally found a vacancy in the old and elegant Hôtel Côte d'Azur. The room was on the fifth and top floor and had a balcony overlooking the avenue, across which was an exquisite little park, and beyond that, the Mediterranean. The room was much too expensive, but as long as she was safe. . . . At least she could pay with Master Charge and save her traveler's checks.

A fifth-floor room seemed a fairly secure place. The only other access would be from the two adjoining balconies, and even that would be difficult. A high fiberglass divider separated each balcony from its neighbor. Any intruder would have to swing perilously around the outside rail, with nothing but air between himself and the busy street.

She moved her luggage from the Foster, but left no for-warding address. Even Steve would not know where to reach her. In a way she regretted it, but better to sacrifice that than leave a trail for Weyland to follow.

But there were the Lanniers. She wandered out onto her balcony in the fresh sunshine, while debating what to do. Would it be presumptuous to call them—presuming that they cared where she was? Or would it be merely polite?

Far out, a white sail caught the sunlight. She closed her eyes against the sparkle of the ocean.

She went back through the sliding glass door and sat down by the telephone. They would probably not be home anyway. Marius would have to report to his office at least once in a while. She put through a call to their home and asked for Madame Lannier.

"Oh, Zhessica!" the older woman gasped with an agitation that left Jessica shocked. "How are you, darling?"

"I'm fine. How are you?"

Madame Lannier murmured a faint "Oh . . ." and Jessica rushed on, still feeling that she was being somewhat pushy, or perhaps irrelevant. "I'll be leaving Nice in a few days, but in the meantime, I've changed my hotel. I just thought I'd let you know the new address. I'm at the Côte d'Azur now, on Avenue de Verdun."

"What? What is that? The what?"

Madame Lannier did not sound in the least like the com-posed, lovely woman of Sunday night. Jessica wondered if she had been drinking.

"The Côte d'Azur. I'm staying at the Côte d'Azur now. It's on the Avenue de Verdun. I thought I should let you know, just in case."

She went on, in an effort to justify herself. "Marius was asking me about something yesterday, so I thought, if he got any more information . . ."

"The Côte d'Azur. I will remember that. Dear Zhessica, you have heard what happened here?"

"What was that? Do you mean about somebody breaking in?"

"No, *no,* oh no, darling, that was nothing. This *morning*." And Madame Lannier began to cry.

Jessica felt a wash of foreboding. "No, what happened?"

"It was *terrible.* The explosion in Marius's car."

"Explosion in Marius's car?"

"The poor girl, she came to borrow his car, and when she tried to start it, the whole thing exploded! It went just like a—"

"Girl?" Jessica asked, her mouth numb and dry. "Do you mean Simone?"

"Yes, yes, Simone. That beautiful girl. Now she is in the hospital and they do not know if she will live."

"Oh, my God."

She wanted to ask how bad it was. But of course it was bad, if they couldn't tell whether Simone would live.

She said, "At least—she's alive." It sounded feeble and stupid. "And Marius? Is he all right?"

"Thank God he was in the house. But how terrible for him, too. My poor Marius."

"Oh, please tell him how sorry I am. If there's anything I can do . . . " Her voice trailed away and the phone clicked in her ear.

Of course there was nothing she could do. She had only said it because she felt so helpless.

Thank God—she echoed what she had just heard—that Marius was safe. But what could have happened? Maybe the radiator . . . no, not a cold radiator. The gas tank. It couldn't be anything else. That was too much.

She drifted back out to the balcony. The sailboat had gone. The sun shone and the water still sparkled, but it looked different now. She barely saw it.

She ought to have left yesterday, gone to Marseilles.

Then she would never have met Simone, and would not have known about this.

She would not have had the ride through the mountains with Marius, or seen the flower farms or the Matisse Chapel.

How could it have happened?

And then she felt ashamed. She was thinking only of the impact on herself, and not of Simone.

The telephone rang. It startled her. Perhaps Madame Lannier had realized, in spite of everything, that she had not said a proper good-bye.

It was Marius.

"Good, you are there. My mother told me you are now in this hotel. I have to see you."

"Of course. Oh, Marius—see me?" She was surprised that, under the circumstances, his mother had even remembered such a trivial fact as Jessica's move.

"It is important. Can you wait for me at two o'clock? In your room?"

"Yes, I'll be here. Marius, I'm so sorry—"

"At two o'clock, then." He hung up.

10

It was twelve-fifteen. Probably too late for the flower market, but she would have time for lunch before he came.

She was closer now to the pedestrian mall, which ran along the block directly in back of the Hôtel Côte d'Azur. She set out, thinking again of the seafood restaurant. As usual, the mall was crowded with tourists and native Niçoises, and the outdoor cafés were already beginning to fill.

Suddenly, without warning, she was surrounded.

There were several of them, young men and women, rough and hard-eyed. One of them reached for her purse.

It was a shoulder bag and it closed with a zipper. Not an easy one to snatch or open. Jessica clung tightly to it and screamed. Instinctively she reached out her foot to stamp on the nearest instep. She felt her heel crunch on flesh and bone.

She thought her resistance would drive them away. Instead they began to jostle her.

"Help!" she screamed. "Gendarmes!"

Heads turned, pale blobs with startled eyes. Not a gendarme was in sight, but the whole rest of the world seemed crowded into that street. How had they dared, with so many people around?

Now that attention was focused on them, her assailants vanished, absorbed by the crowd.

A man with an elaborate camera bag asked in broad American, "Are you okay?"

"I'm fine," she said, feeling the weakness of relief. "They tried to take my purse."

A woman inquired, "Are you all right? Do you want me to get the police for you?"

"I don't see what they can do," Jessica replied.

"You ought to report these things."

She did not know where to find the police. Besides, it would take time, and she might not get back to her hotel by two o'clock.

As they started away, the man said, "Keep a grip on that purse."

She abandoned her more elaborate plans, reached the pizza café, and sat down at a vacant table. She still felt disturbed and no longer hungry, but supposed she would be hungry later if she did not eat.

While she waited to be served, she thought over what had happened, replaying it in slow motion. Could she have been more careful?

She kept seeing the whole thing, their faces, the one tough-looking woman, a thin and wiry man with large hands, and another who seemed almost familiar, but that was impossible.

What if they had succeeded? She would have lost her passport and all her money, her traveler's checks. She would be left with nothing.

Thank God, she thought for the second time that day.

By the time Marius knocked at her door, she had fully recovered. She had not been hurt and nothing was stolen. Her concern now was for Simone.

He came in, carrying a white plastic bag and frowning slightly, as though his mind was far away.

"How is she?" Jessica asked.

"How is—?" He looked at her blankly for a moment,

94

and then his face cleared. "Simone?" He wandered across the room. A glass-topped table stood near the balcony door, with an orange upholstered chair beside it. He gestured for her to sit down, then seated himself in a straight-backed chair from the desk against the wall.

"It is very bad," he said. "Fortunately it is not—how to say it? She is a beautiful woman, and that is not destroyed, her face. But they had to cut her hair, because she had injuries on the head."

"Then she's not—mutilated?"

It sounded horrible. She was not even sure he would understand, but he did, and she remembered that the French word was similar.

"No, in that she is all right. She is more hurt on the inside. I don't know how she can be all right. A bomb explosion—"

"A *bomb*?"

"Yes, that is why I want to talk. But I want to see you without the police, because of the things you say about Henri, who is my friend. I want to know more about this first. Without the police."

He opened the bag he had brought and took out a bottle of rosé wine and a package of plastic tumblers. "We will soften these troubles a little bit," he explained. "Please excuse that we haven't got wine glasses. I did not want to ask the hotel and let anyone know that I am here."

He poured wine for each of them and then looked around at the room and the view.

"This is a very nice place, but why do you move?"

She explained why she had moved, and it did indeed begin to sound neurotic. Nothing that happened had been very unusual, except the incident with Weyland, but that had taken place outside the hotel. To add a little more urgency to her story, she told him about the gang that had menaced her that day on the pedestrian mall.

95

"I really love your city," she added, "but sometimes I have to work at loving it. I don't know why these things keep happening. Unless it's all part of the same thing."

He seemed to be only half listening. "They were young? Teenagers?"

"They were young, but grown up. One of them had a beard. They looked like—" She could not explain. "I mean, they were tough and unfriendly, but they didn't look like the sort of people—well, I don't know."

He shrugged. "Nice is a popular place for the tourists. These things can happen. Only you must be careful."

"Oh, I understand all that, about tourists and vultures, but why pick me? I don't even look rich. And with so many people around, it really was brazen."

"Sometimes a crowd is the best concealment," he said.

She sipped her wine. It was light and semisweet.

"Anyway, that really isn't important, when poor Simone—"

"Yes," he agreed, his attention fully recaptured. "That is a mystery, why it happened. I did not say it to my mother, but I think it might have something to do with Françoise, and what you tell me about Henri."

"With Françoise? You don't think your friend—"

"That I do not know. But I told you, I had some questions about what she was doing even before she went to the United States. She goes to the secret meetings, talks quietly on the telephone, and then she comes and tells me that a friend of hers is starting the export business. She does not say who the friend is, but she wants some advice. I ask her what is he exporting. She won't tell me. I introduce her to someone I know, to get the advice. Later he tells me it came to nothing, they wanted to ship the painted dishes, but they have not enough money to start the business.

"Then she is killed," he went on. "I accepted the police statement, but when you came with this story about

96

Henri and what is happening, and how he went to visit Françoise only a few days before she is killed, what am I to think?"

"So it's because I came," she said. "That's why these things have been happening. Before you and I met each other, neither of us knew anything, but when I put my story together with yours, it could add up to something. I suppose that's why Weyland—I mean Henri—was upset when he found out I'd met you."

He closed his eyes. Obviously that was something he dreaded.

"So it is first Henri," he said. "We must start there. But we have to be certain that this is the same man you saw."

"I'm almost sure it is. That picture you had, could I see it again?"

He was wearing a suit with pockets and had not brought the black leather bag, but he did have the pictures, deliberately, she supposed. Again she studied the one of Henri with his tennis racket. There was no doubt in her mind that he was Weyland.

"Unless he has a twin brother," she said.

"Not Henri. But I wonder about him. He has been away very much. He is, you see, the way he works, a special kind of chemist. He works for my mother, but he has his own laboratory because he does other things, too. He has his own things that he is working on."

"Things that have nothing to do with perfume?"

Marius nodded. "I don't know what they are. He is free to do as he likes. He buys his own chemicals and uses the laboratory when he is not working for the factory. We do not ask questions what he does. And sometimes he goes away for awhile. Now we can't find him, not at home, not at the factory."

"But he found me."

"Yes, but why does he talk to you this way? He talks about Françoise, yes? And he tells you not to see me. We

97

know Françoise was killed, but here I am wondering, what has that to do with you, and with me, unless someone is afraid we will find out what has happened? It seems, you see, that the bomb was meant for me. Only by chance was Simone in my car instead of me."

"But if Simone wasn't killed," Jessica speculated, "maybe they didn't mean to kill you. If Henri did it, and he's your friend, maybe he only wanted to frighten you, so you'd stop investigating."

He shook his head. "The police think, if it was me, I would have been killed. But Simone is lighter weight. She was thrown a little way, and probably that saved her."

With great calm, considering what had befallen his Simone, he refilled their wine glasses, then settled back, holding his up to the light.

"Maybe this is a strange thing to do," he asked, "to bring the wine to your room?"

"Oh, no, it's lovely. It seems kind of—American, almost, except we'd probably drink beer. But I like this. It's good wine."

"I'm glad you approve of my choice. Now, Zhessica, here is another question. When you met Claude Augustín at the factory, you said he reminded you of someone. Have you a chance yet to remember who it is?"

"No, I really haven't been thinking about it. I didn't know it was important."

"It is important. The person to whom I introduced Françoise, when she wanted help with her exporting business, is Claude Augustín."

"Oh. I see. But couldn't you find out from him what was going on?"

"I have asked, and he says she wanted only to export the dishes, whatever you call it, the pottery. It is all he knows. But this, I think, would not turn out to be dangerous for her."

"I should hardly think so. And you're wondering if it really was dishes."

"Yes, I am wondering."

"I'll try to remember if I've seen him. But I really don't think—I mean, I don't forget faces that easily. He probably just reminds me of someone."

"He did not visit the college?"

"No, I don't *think*—Marius, I just remembered something. This has nothing to do with Mr. Augustín, but Weyland asked if Françoise had given me anything. The only thing she gave me was a picture. I didn't tell him about it, because I didn't want him to think I was involved in any way. As far as I can see, there's nothing special about the picture, it's just Françoise and some man. Maybe it will mean something to you." She unzipped her suitcase and took out her purse.

"Why do you keep your handbag in there?" he asked.

"In the suitcase? So if a maid comes in, or somebody, they won't see it."

"But you are here."

"Yes, but I might not be watching all the time. It just makes me feel better."

He took the picture from her. "Who is this man?"

"I don't know. He doesn't show up well. He doesn't look very specific. No, that's a funny thing to say about a person—but he doesn't. That mustache, the nose . . . It could be anybody."

She stood behind him and looked at the picture over his shoulder. There was something about the way the man held his head. He looked almost like one of the mannequins Eileen Fowler had borrowed and Françoise had dressed. It was a ludicrous image. The idea was to make mannequins look like people, not the other way around.

"What did she talk about?" Marius asked.

"About everything, I guess. Or do you mean her ideas? Well, she wanted to do things, change things. In a way, she was sort of radical. It happens a lot of times. People who grow up having everything...Maybe they've had it all given to them, never had to work for it, and they feel useless and unimportant. So they take up a cause."

"Did Françoise have a cause?" He seemed to be asking the question of himself. "The secret meetings, and the way she changed, and now the bomb, if that has to do with her."

"And Weyland."

"And Henri. It does not sound to me like an ordinary exporting business. But, Zhessica, what was it? Do you remember if she said anything about it?"

"Not so it made sense. Just little things now and then. 'When I started it, I never knew it would be like this.' That sort of thing. It was vague. And it all had to do with someone who I think was important to her."

Absently he rubbed his chin and stared at the rug.

"She was going to be married at one time," he said slowly, "to a man named Charles, who now lives in Cannes, where he is working. But Françoise changed her mind."

"She never mentioned anyone named Charles."

"No, that was finished, I think. And poor Charles, then he fell in love with Simone."

"Simone? The one who was—"

"Yes, the one who was hurt in my car."

"Poor Simone," Jessica said. Whatever envy she may have felt had turned to horror and pity for that lovely, vital girl who cared so much about the impression she made that she even dressed her dog to match.

"I hope the dog wasn't hurt."

He looked startled, then smiled faintly. "No, the dog was not with her. She had an important errand, and I said she could use my car. She was going to take me to my office. First she wanted to see if she could start the car and drive it."

"Poor girl," Jessica said again, and added, "but she'll be all right, won't she?"

"If she is not, I will never forgive myself, since it was meant for me."

"But it's not your fault!"

His own absolution was not as easy as hers. "How do I know it is not my fault? I have not any idea what this thing is about. Zhessica, we must find the person who you say was important to Françoise."

He picked up the photograph, which had been resting on his knee, and looked at it again.

"Where is this place?"

"It's the college," she said. "I don't know if you saw it when you were there. A very small college, only about four hundred students. I thought I knew everybody, at least by sight, but that man— He might have been someone who visited her, or someone from the village of Fort Sheffield. I think this was—" Again she was assailed by a feeling of unreality, a feeling that the man himself was not real. But only because his clothes resembled those on the mannequins, and that was natural. It had been an international fair and many people had come in costume.

"I think it was taken during the fair I told you about. That's the corner of our dormitory building, and there's Françoise's window. She always had those books piled on her windowsill."

He studied the photograph, then turned it over and looked at the back. He frowned, and swung toward the balcony door for better light.

"There was something written here," he said. "It was rubbed out, but you can see where it pressed down. Have you a pencil, Zhessica, with a long point?"

"I have a pencil, but the point's not very long. I don't have a sharpener." She opened her suitcase once more, took out the spiral notebook in which she was trying to keep her diary, and removed a pencil from inside the binding.

He used the side of the lead, rather than the end of it, and carefully shaded the back of the picture until the grooves where the words had been showed up white under the darkened foreground.

He was unsuccessful in the first and perhaps most important part of the inscription. It might have been the man's name, for the rest of the phrase was *et moi*. And me. Below it was written *Danger! Danger! Danger!*

Marius whispered the message to himself, giving the word its French pronunciation.

"This might be what we are looking for," he said. "It is hard to know. Maybe she is only teasing with her 'danger.' But if she is afraid of this man, why does she stand with him to have her picture taken?"

"Maybe the picture was taken before— But it couldn't have been. The fair was in early April, and there was hardly any time after that."

Any time for Françoise, was what she meant. And yet that might have been exactly why Françoise gave her the picture.

She was still formulating her thoughts, when Marius said, "Then this is where we start. We must find out more about it. But to do that, I suppose we have to go to the United States. Still, it puzzles me. What has this to do with Henri?"

He turned to her as he spoke. Their eyes met and she looked away quickly.

"It's strange," she said. "If Françoise knew—I mean, why would she give the picture to me? If she thought something was going to happen, and she wanted—"

"To leave a message? Maybe she thought it would be safe with you. If she left it in her room, perhaps the killer would find it first."

"Weyland—Henri—asked if anyone had been in her room. That was one of the things yesterday, when he— talked to me."

Marius smiled wryly as he rose to leave.

"So we must find Henri. But I think he is hiding. He comes only to you."

"I hope he doesn't do it often."

"Yes, you must be careful, Zhessica. I don't want you to get hurt."

"That's nice of you, but remember, you're the one they tried to kill."

He waved his hand, dismissing the danger. "Zhessica, I have thought of something. May I take the picture for a little while to see if I can find out anything more? I will give it back to you."

"Of course. Keep it as long as you want."

They both reached for the picture, which lay on the glass-topped table. Their hands and then their bodies brushed each other. Marius picked up the picture and slipped it into his pocket. Jessica tried to move away, but he caught her with his arm around her waist and pulled her close to him. His lips touched her forehead, and then, with a casual wave, he was gone, closing the door after himself.

11

By the time he left, it was midafternoon. She hardly dared go out, but she had not come to Nice to spend her time imprisoned in a hotel room.

Perhaps the beach. It was busy enough. If Weyland really was in hiding, he would scarcely want to make such a public appearance. She packed her bag with towel and bathing suit and set off for the private beach, hoping that even the small entrance fee might be a deterrent to anyone following her.

The umbrellas were all rented. Only mattresses were available. She lay in the hot sunshine, thinking of Marius, and trying not to think of Marius. A light, brotherly kiss from a Frenchman was certainly not to be taken seriously. And there was Simone, lying smashed in the hospital.

She contemplated her own ridiculousness. Who would follow her to the beach, and why?

But Weyland had pursued her before, and captured her, and there was that picture of Françoise with its legend of danger.

After an hour, she began to feel herself burning despite liberal doses of suntan cream. She left the beach and, wandering up a side street, found a small grocery store, where she bought bread, cheese, and wine.

When the sun was lower and her balcony had cooled, she ate her supper overlooking the sea. The only distraction was the sound of traffic and swarms of motorcycles on the Avenue de Verdun below her. Would she ever see the rest of Nice, the Old Town and the flower market? Even this afternoon, when there was time, she had been afraid. The streets of the Old Town were small and tightly packed, and she could be followed. He might be there, waiting for her.

She remained on the balcony, writing a letter to her parents. So much had happened, but there was little she could tell them.

> Today I changed my hotel. It made me just a little bit nervous, having the tree outside my window.

Her father would approve of that precaution.

> Sunday I leave for Marseilles, and after that, Aix. I always wanted to see a town with a name like Aix-en-Provence. It has hot springs where people go for their health, and the picture in my guidebook shows a perfectly gorgeous old street. Plenty of history, anyway.

She folded the letter, sealed and stamped it, and then took a long, soaking bath.

Marius. . . . Was he really on the trail of his sister's killer? Was that what the killer feared, and was that why he had planted the bomb? But if that was the killer in the picture, he should have been thousands of miles away, in Fort Sheffield, New York.

She finished her bath and settled in bed with the copy of *L'Express,* which she had bought and not yet looked at.

She could get the drift of it, if not every word. It was almost flattering, the attention that Europeans paid to American politics, although the things they said about it were frequently patronizing, if not downright derogatory. And yet they were hardly ones to talk, for they had a checkered history of their own.

On the next page, devastation. A lake of crude oil in the desert. Pipeline exploded by Moslem guerrillas from San'a, the caption said. She wondered where San'a was, and could not comprehend what Moslem guerrillas would have to gain by exploding a pipeline. Or why the human race always had to be fighting.

The article ran on to the next page and included a map. An X marked the site of the explosion, somewhere in northern Saudi Arabia, a long way from San'a, which turned out to be the capital of North Yemen. The guerrillas claimed they were waging a holy war against the godless Communists, who had gotten their claws into South Yemen. *Pravda* called it a war of imperialist aggression, backed by the CIA, and vowed it would be smashed.

Yemen.

Aden.

Eagerly she studied the map. She knew there was a North and a South Yemen, but could not remember which was which. Aden, the capital of South Yemen. People's Yemen. The Marxist one.

The exploded pipeline . . .

No, she thought, that's too far-fetched. And he wouldn't be *here,* what would he be doing here?

He lives here.

She reached for the telephone, but withdrew her hand. It was too late at night. She would have to remember what Weyland had said, what he had talked about. She had mostly thought of herself, and the fact that Françoise was dead, and soon she would be, too.

He had said there was "too much at stake."

But it could have been anything, depending upon what he considered important.

Gradually she ran down, like a wound-up clock. Marius

must already have thought of this, and rejected it, for one reason or another. She would not call him now. Maybe tomorrow morning, just to mention it.

She read the article again, and the map. Did Weyland really come from there? She supposed that, as a British colony and important seaport, it must have been a crossroads, a possible place for an adventurous young Frenchwoman to meet and marry an aristocratic Yemenite some thirty or thirty-five years ago. Or perhaps they had met in Paris, Nice, or Monte Carlo.

The most extraordinary part of all was that eventually Jessica's own life should be touched by it.

But still, it was a shrinking world, as the clichés pointed out, and no man or woman was an island, entire of itself.

Any man's death diminishes me, because I am involved in mankind; and therefore never send to know for whom the bell tolls; it tolls for thee.

She lay staring at the wall, with tears in her eyes, thinking of Françoise. Of Simone. And even the young Frenchwoman and the Yemenite, and the tiny band of guerrillas recklessly fighting the giant Red war machine.

Odd, she thought, how these obscure places suddenly become headlines.

After a while the tears went away. She turned another page, struggled through a short item on South Africa, and topped it off with a dessert of movie reviews.

So much for the French lesson. It had been a success, but not a resounding one. Her pocket dictionary contained too small a vocabulary to be useful for *L'Express*. It was only ten o'clock, but for lack of anything else to do, she turned off her light and closed her eyes.

She had always been a light sleeper. The smallest disturbance, even a change in barometric pressure, would wake her. "A born mother," her own mother had told her hopefully. "You'll wake at every whimper. It's good to be alert."

She had not known that she was alert that night, had not even known that something woke her, until the layers of sleep fell away and she was staring into darkness, trying to orient herself.

The next instant it all came clear, where she was and what had awakened her, for she was looking through the door to her balcony, and someone was out there.

She screamed. Her shrieks split the air, but she barely heard them. As she jumped from her bed and ran to the hall door, the figure vanished.

How?

She thought it had gone to the left. Her left. It took her a moment to gather enough courage to creep toward the balcony and look out.

It was empty. The avenue below hummed with its usual traffic, and an occasional siren.

Cautiously she peered around the fiberglass divider. The adjoining balcony was also empty. The door into the room was open, and the room dark.

She hurried back inside, closed the balcony door and locked it. She lowered the blind.

Could they have taken the room next to hers? Could they have been so bold? Or desperate?

She turned on a lamp and telephoned the hotel desk. Within minutes, a man and a woman arrived at her door.

Upon hearing her story, the man clasped his hands. "Oh, mademoiselle, it is impossible. The people in that room, they are respectable, not so young, a man and a woman from Sweden. How would they do such a thing?"

"I don't know how," Jessica said, "but there was someone on my balcony, and I don't know where he could have come from or gone to, except one of the other rooms."

"But how could he cross over?" the man wanted to know. "It is *dangereux*. He would fall into the street."

Clearly implying that the elderly Swedish couple, even had they wanted, could not have managed the climb.

She did not suspect the Swedish couple of anything. "What about the room beyond it?"

"Two lady doctors from Paris."

She was sure the figure had gone to the left, but not leaving anything to chance, asked about the room on her right. An American, the man informed her, a college professor. Also not young.

"Perhaps it was a bad dream?" he suggested.

"I know it must seem that way," she told him, remembering that at the Foster they had treated her the same way, "but it was not a dream. Unless I'm still dreaming, and you're part of it. There *was* someone out there."

She was on the brink of telling him about her intruder at the Foster, but thought better of it. Either he would conclude that she was hopelessly paranoid, or be angry with her for bringing her troubles to his hotel.

With extreme reluctance, he went to knock on the Swedish couple's door, while his female companion, who spoke no English, remained with Jessica and from time to time flashed her a mischievous smile. If there had been a prowler, the woman seemed to think, it must have been someone Jessica knew, and she was only spoiling the fun with her uproar.

Jessica heard voices in the hallway, and the man returned. "They have heard nothing and seen nothing," he reported. "There was no stranger in their room. So I would suggest that you rest assured this hotel is secure, and go back to sleep. It will all seem better in the morning. *Bonne nuit,* mam'selle."

She nodded to him as he left, but did not thank him, and afterward felt ashamed. She was beginning to doubt herself, and what more could he have done except search every room in the hotel, with the nimble intruder, meanwhile, getting farther and farther away? If there had even been an intruder.

The room was miserably stuffy with the balcony door

closed. It was also dark with the blind down, so that when she turned out the lamp, she was in total blackness, without an up or a down.

She wondered whether the lock on the door was secure. And what about the hallway door, even with her burglar alarm rigged to it?

She closed her eyes and felt the air press in around her.

Had she really seen someone out there? Or had she only expected to?

12

In the morning she examined her balcony for any signs of a prowler. She found nothing but a spot where paint was chipped off the railing, and it might have been that way all along.

How could he have swung over the divider, and then back again? It could not have been anyone but an acrobat.

A soft breeze blew across her face. She lifted her head and the prowler receded, at least for the time being. It was a new morning. The air was fresh and hazy and the sky bright, although the sun was momentarily hidden behind a drift of blue and yellow clouds. From the haze, she knew that as soon as the sun reappeared, it would be another warm day.

In the park directly opposite the hotel, men were raking the grass and watering the bushes. One, high on a ladder, sawed the dead leaves from a date palm. The sun's rays began to shine from behind the clouds.

She went down to the hotel dining room, ate her usual breakfast of rolls and croissant, and then waited at the front desk for the concierge. As soon as he arrived, she asked for another room.

He remembered her from the day before. His eyes widened. "Another room? But that is a beautiful room. You are very fortunate, miss."

Evidently the night people had not told him of the disturbance. She described what had happened, and met the same wall of disbelief.

But he was polite about it.

"I am sorry, miss. We will look into the matter, but as for another room, I cannot help you. We have no more available. There are the tour groups, you see. Three tour groups in this hotel. It was only by great good fortune that we could give you a room at all. And such a beautiful one."

She took the elevator back to her beautiful room. She could, after all, cut short her trip and just go home.

But this was the trip of her lifetime. She might never have another chance. And what would she tell her parents?

As she unlocked the door to her room, she heard the telephone ringing.

Her first thought was Marius.

Then it occurred to her that it might be a trap to catch her unaware. She glanced in the bathroom, the wardrobe, and under the bed before she closed the door and picked up the still-ringing phone.

"You are there?" Marius asked in surprise. "I was ready to give up."

"I just got in," she told him breathlessly. "I was trying to change my room. There was someone on the balcony last night."

"Yes?" He sounded skeptical.

"They didn't believe me, and they had no other rooms. But anyway, that's what I was doing."

"I don't understand," he said, "how anyone could get to your balcony."

"Maybe it was all a dream. The kind that dissipates just as you're waking up." She laughed shortly. How could she expect him to be concerned about a shadow on her balcony, when Simone had been struck by a very real bomb? "How is Simone?"

"She is a little better. I went to visit her last night. She is not so confused any more, and can talk better. She still does not quite know what happened. I don't want to tell her yet. And how are you, Zhessica? You did not sleep well with this trouble on your balcony?"

"No, I didn't. After I shut and locked the door, it was so stuffy I couldn't breathe."

"You have, I think, the air conditioning in your room, no?"

"I suppose so." She hadn't thought of air conditioning. There had been none at the Foster. "I didn't know where to turn it on. Marius, I got to thinking—"

Another cautious "Yes?" She wondered if he suspected that someone might be listening.

"I got to thinking, maybe it would be better for everybody if I just left. There's no real reason for me to stay in Nice, and your troubles only started when I came. Nobody bothered me in Paris, and nobody—"

"You will leave Nice?" It seemed to shock him.

"I think it's the only thing to do, don't you? I haven't seen the Old Town yet, or that mountain they call the Château, but it can't be helped."

"Wait, Zhessica, I must talk to you again. I will come there in an hour. Is it all right? Do you have the time?"

"Time? That's all I have."

And maybe that was all she wanted to do with it. There was still tomorrow for the Old Town, the flower market, and her shopping.

She was wearing yellow slacks with a flowered blouse, and considered changing to a dress. But that would look so obvious, as though she had done it for him. She was not, after all, Simone. She kept the yellow slacks on and went out again to her balcony, still certain that she had seen someone, but not understanding how.

It occurred to her that perhaps the fiberglass divider could be moved. She tugged and pushed, but it was firmly bolted in place. The bolts, in fact, were quite visible.

She looked around and found herself staring, first at the white metal table with its two matching chairs, and then at the overhang from the roof above it.

Her room was on the top floor. The roof, she knew, contained an outdoor lounge where people could order drinks and snacks. A stairway led up to it from the fifth floor. Anyone could go up there, and if the door was locked at night, anyone could remain there, hidden behind a wall or a potted tree. An agile and nerveless person could drop down onto her balcony, and if need be, hoist himself up again by standing on the table. It was a single-pedestal table; she would have been terrified, but then, she was not nerveless. And that was why he had seemed to go to the left, because that was where the table was.

He, or she. It didn't matter. What mattered was that they could reach her even here.

And she could not change her room.

She locked the balcony door tightly, as she would have to lock it at night, and turned on the air conditioner, the controls for which she found easily enough, now that Marius had mentioned it.

She was notified of his arrival by a call from the house phone downstairs.

"Bring your handbag and your camera," he told her. "Whatever you need for a trip today. That is, if you still have no other plans. I will be outside in my mother's car."

Once she was safely in the car, he told her their itinerary.

"We are going first to Cannes, to see the man Charles that I told you about, who was planning once to marry Françoise. She might have talked more to him than to me. That is all right? I wanted you with me. We can try to put everything together."

"Yes, it's fine. I'd like to see Cannes. Marius, I found out how the person got onto my balcony. From the roof."

"So you really did see someone. You must be careful, Zhessica. Maybe you should move into our house."

"Oh, I couldn't. I might make it worse for you."

"Or we might make it worse for you. So far, they have not tried to bomb you. But we will have to think of something. That is bad, if they can get into your room."

"It's quite likely," she said, "that they wouldn't try it again, at least not that way, since I saw them last night. And I'll lock the door."

"I don't like it," he said.

"I don't much, either. But I'll be gone in a few days. Maybe they won't follow me to Marseilles."

She watched the tourists in bright sports clothes crossing the boulevard to the beaches. Every beach was marked with festive, fluttering banners, while in the calm and incredibly blue water, people swam, or sailed, or in cosy twosomes, lazily propelled small pedal boats.

This was what the Côte d'Azur should have been for her. This peace and innocence.

"Marius," she said, "do you know there's a war going on in Yemen?"

He took time to absorb the information before he answered, "A little war."

"I guess it's hardly even a war right now, until the Russians send in troops. They're not going to give up easily on that piece of the Arabian Peninsula."

"No, I suppose not."

"I was reading about it last night in *L'Express*. I almost called you, but then I thought it probably wasn't news to you."

"Why didn't you call me?" he asked with a smile. "It would have been a pleasure."

"I'm sure it would, but I couldn't see bothering you at that hour with such a silly thing."

"War is not silly, Zhessica."

"No, I didn't mean that. I meant it was silly because

115

obviously it's something you would have thought of yourself."

"I know what you are saying," he told her. "I have seen
about it in the newspapers. But you must understand,
Henri has long been away from Aden. I have thought of it,
but I did not see where it would take us. I don't understand what that would have to do with Françoise. Or you
or me. Or why Simone is now in the hospital."

She nodded. It did seem rather extreme, for something
so remote. But Françoise had clearly been involved in
something more than a simple business venture.

She said, "I didn't know Françoise was mixed up in anything. She seemed so—"

"She was very mixed up," he agreed.

"No, I mean—I didn't know she was into anything. I
knew she seemed passionate about her ideas, and they
sometimes struck me as a little belligerent, but her earnest-
ness was kind of cute. I thought she was entitled to her
own opinions, as long as she didn't do anything belligerent."

"I wonder why—" he began. "It was in August last
year, all of a sudden she decides to go to the United States.
She gives no reason except to study, but she wants very
much to go. Almost as if she is trying to get away. I
thought, at the time, maybe it is the love affair."

"Do you mean the man we're going to see?"

"No, that was long before. Another one, but I didn't
really know. It is only that I can think of no other reason
why a young woman should want to get away. That is, at
the time. Now it is different."

"But you still don't know what it is."

"No, I don't. Only that you and I are both in trouble.
You brought your pieces of the puzzle and added them to
mine, and this way we might be able to find the whole.
And that they have done to themselves. If they would go
away someplace else, and Henri keeps out of the picture so

116

I never learn from you that he was with Françoise in the United States, maybe I would still think Françoise died from a robber. But now—"

"I guess he couldn't help it," she said. "I really don't think he intended for me to see him when he was coming here. And I did tell you about him before he got me into his car. It's just that we couldn't identify him."

He muttered, "There must be another reason."

"What is your friend going to do?" she asked. "The one in Cannes."

"For one thing, he is going with us to Grasse and he will bring back Simone's car. I have asked them to call a mechanic and get it fixed. But I thought of Charles, not only would he be willing, but also he knew Françoise very well at the time she was becoming interested in these new activities. That I think is what ended the engagement. Maybe he can tell us what the activities were."

They drove in silence for a while, through the ancient town of Antibes, then the green and shady Juan-les-Pins. Marius seemed absorbed in thought, and only emerged from it now and then to tell her where they were.

He might have been thinking of Simone. Perhaps he believed that if Jessica had not come, bringing Henri's wrath on her trail, none of these things would have happened. Of course he would want to find his sister's killer, but was it worth the danger to innocent people?

He glanced at his watch. "We are too early for Charles. Would you like to have dinner?"

"Dinner?" she asked blankly. Dinner was at seven o'clock, after the store closed.

"Or whatever you call it. On that other trip to Grasse, I forgot that we must eat."

"A strange omission for a Frenchman, but I didn't mind. I wasn't hungry. Is this Cannes?"

"We are coming to it."

As in Nice, they were driving along a boulevard that ran

by the shore. "It's beautiful!" she exclaimed. The median mall was planted with trees and pink petunias. Beyond it, bordering the shore itself, was a park, cool and leafy, bright with oleander bushes and red, pink, and white flower beds.

"What's that island out there?"

"Those," he said, "are the Îles de Lérins. They are two, Saint-Honorat and Sainte-Marguerite. Brother and sister."

"Brother and—sister?" How often he must think of Françoise. She wondered if a person could ever get used to losing someone so close.

"They lived in the fourth century," he told her. "Saint Honorat built a monastery on his island, and Marguerite had a convent on the other. She wanted to see her brother sometimes, but women were not allowed in the monastery, and only he could go to her. But he was busy with his prayers and he told her he would come once a year, when the almond tree was in flower. Marguerite was so unhappy that she prayed to God, and then an almond tree that was near the shore began to have flowers every month."

"That's a lovely story. You know so much, you could write a book on Provence."

He looked at her and smiled. "I am not a writer, I am a businessman. And I think there are already many books on Provence, no?"

"I suppose there are. But it's such a fascinating place."

He asked, "Do you mind to eat in a cafeteria? It is not elegant, but is quick."

The only thing she minded was that all this must pass. She had almost forgotten the danger.

He searched for a parking place, and when the car was disposed of, led her to a cafeteria with a tree-shaded terrace that faced the boulevard and the shore.

When they had selected their lunches and were seated at a table in a corner of the terrace, Marius nodded to a pier directly opposite them.

"From there you can take a boat to the Îles de Lérins. It is too bad we have no time today. If you would stay in Nice for a little while, perhaps another time—"

"I think I've stayed in Nice too long as it is," she said. "I never should have come here, but I didn't know, then."

"What has happened," he said, "may have happened anyway, we don't know. Maybe you think, Zhessica, that I am foolish to leave my work for another day and go again to Grasse, but I have a reason. Not only to get Simone's car, that is a very minor reason. There is something I am trying to find out, something that may have to do with Françoise. I find out very quietly, but I think maybe when you came here, it stirred things up a little bit."

"A little bit!"

"Or maybe very much. I am watching, and probably I am right. That is why I want to go to Grasse."

"Does it have to do with the picture?"

"I don't know. It has to do with Françoise, I think. As for the picture, maybe that is not what these people want from you, although it is certain that they want something. Maybe some information. Something that was slipped to you, and you don't know you have it."

"I thought of that, too," she said, "but I don't remember anything being slipped to me. I still think they wanted to scare me away from you. And I should have listened."

"You are not eating, Zhessica."

"I guess I forgot." She looked at her plate, which contained a breaded veal cutlet and an enormous pile of fried potatoes. On the side was a small, artistically arranged egg salad.

"That's a lot of French fries," she said. "Will you think I'm wasteful if I don't eat them all?"

"French fries? What is that? The *pommes frites*?"

"Oh, I forgot. This *is* France. We call them French fried potatoes. I suppose you invented them, or something. Or maybe it's because—" She gestured toward her plate, "with every meal in France—every meal—you get an absolute mountain of them."

He smiled. "Not in the fine restaurants. Only the cafés. I see you have not been eating well. Before you leave Nice, I must take you to a good restaurant."

"Actually, I exaggerated a little," she apologized. "At least with pizza, they don't give you French fries."

"*Pizza?* Ah, Zhessica, why do you come to France?"

"To see France. Not to eat."

"But that is part of seeing France, no? And here in the Côte d'Azur we have our own special cuisine. You must try them all, the *specialité* of every place."

"You did take me to a nice restaurant in Villefranche," she reminded him. "But please don't tell me to eat like that every day. I couldn't afford it."

She wondered if he even knew what it was like to have limited money.

He was silent for a while, and then asked, "But why is it that you are so interested in France? Is it because of Françoise?"

"I'm interested in all of Europe. But I wanted to start with France, and especially Nice, because of Françoise."

"Did she know you were planning to come here?"

"Oh, yes, I had my plane reservation in March. She told me I ought to meet you."

He withdrew into thought again, while she chopped at her *pommes frites* with her fork. She had finished eating. They were only passing the time.

"Then," he said, "she had a reason for giving you the picture. That is what I hope to find out today. The reason."

13

They returned to the car and wound through the business section of Cannes. Stopping before a small office building, Marius left her and disappeared inside. A few minutes later he returned with a blond young man whose mustache topped a gleaming smile.

Marius introduced his friend. "This is Charles Roussillon." She heard her own name in the midst of French phrases, then Marius returned to English. "I am sorry to leave you alone in the car. It is forbidden to park here, and I thought if the police come and see a pretty girl, they will not give me a ticket. Also, I did not know it would take Charles so long to be ready."

"Telephone," Charles explained in extremely limited English. Or perhaps it was French. The smile did not diminish.

"If you two want to talk," Jessica offered, stepping out of the car, "I could sit in back."

Marius appeared disconcerted, but after a moment of reflection, grateful.

"Is it all right, Zhessica? I'm sorry, it is nicer to see from the front, but I must find out what he knows about Françoise. We can save time if we talk in the car."

She heard Charles let out a sigh about "belle Simone" as they started off. Soon the conversation switched to Françoise.

Marius looked back at her briefly. "Did she have any men friends at the university?"

"Friends, yes," Jessica said, "but nothing romantic. Except—I thought—Henri—"

"We do not know about Henri. He is a big question."

"She had some visitors, I remember. One night I saw her having dinner with two men. They were all speaking French."

"What did they look like?"

"It was hard to tell. They both had mustaches, and one had a beard. He was older, I think, the one with the beard."

"What do you mean? How much older?"

"Maybe, I don't know, forties or fifties. He couldn't have been too old, his hair wasn't gray."

"When did this happen?"

"Sometime in the winter. I can't remember exactly when."

"That is interesting," he said, and turned back to Charles. They reverted to French, and she stared out of the window, trying to understand what they were talking about. She heard the name "Henri" several times, and again "Françoise," but they spoke too fast for her.

A warm wind blew against her face, although nothing stirred the leaves on the trees or the weeds by the roadside. She could imagine people in centuries past bringing their rheumatic bodies from the north to bake in this sunshine, seasoned with the hot smell of herbs and wildflowers. It was a heat that could flatten a person, but also breathe life.

Marius half turned his head. The road was winding into the mountains, past bare white rocks and bristling pine trees.

"It seems," he said, "that you are right. Charles says that after Françoise and he were finished, there was Henri. She told Charles only that there was someone else. He

122

learned by accident that it was Henri. Then, if she was in love with him, why doesn't she tell anyone? Why so much secret?"

"Maybe he's married?" Jessica asked.

"Not as far as I know. Did she say nothing to you about Henri?"

"She never mentioned him. And she acted very secretive when I discovered him."

"You discovered him? How?"

"Well, I mean—she had her door shut, and I knocked and then I started to open it. We always did that with each other. It was usually all right. But when I pushed it open, a chair fell over, so I backed out. Then she came and invited me in. I thought Weyland—Henri—at first looked angry. I had the impression that she was trying to minimize—to make it less important than it was. *I* didn't care if she wanted a man in her room."

"You are being very helpful, Zhessica. Yes, we must follow this business of Henri. Zhessica, will you show Charles the picture you have of Françoise?"

"But you have it," she reminded him. "You asked to borrow it, remember?"

"Yes, you are right. I'm sorry." He spoke to Charles, who opened the zippered bag on the front seat and withdrew the folder of pictures. Jessica leaned forward to point out the one they meant. As Charles studied it, there was much discussion about "l'homme," and the inscription on the back.

Charles seemed to think the man was Henri. Jessica tried to explain, in halting French, that Henri was shorter and heavier, and his head a different shape.

"No, no," said Charles, and elaborated incomprehensibly.

Marius translated. "He says it is the haircut and the shadows in the picture that make him look different. And, of course, the mustache. You are sure it is not one of the men you saw with her at dinner?"

"Not the older one, anyway. I just don't know. I only saw them for a minute. As for Henri, he didn't have a mustache when he was there, and the picture would have to be taken there, because of the dormitory. Did you find out any way to read the name on the back, before *'et moi'*?"

"I have tried," said Marius. "There is no way that I know to do it."

"Some chemical, maybe?"

"We have chemists at the factory—including, of course, Henri. Unfortunately their specialty is the perfume, not the pencil lead. However, we will try. I have asked one of them to meet us."

They were nearing the factory. She recognized the mountain that rose straight ahead of them, before the turnoff in the road.

Again, as recklessly as before, he spun onto the narrow approach, past the two stone farmhouses, and then into the shady parking lot of the factory.

Parfums Broucard seemed to dance in the heat of the afternoon. Simone's car stood where she had left it. A yellow leaf had fallen onto its roof.

No tour buses were in sight. It was a quiet day.

As they walked toward the building, a young man in blue jeans came from the main door and spoke to Marius, who raised his hands in helpless surprise.

"This man," Marius explained, "says they called a mechanic, and there is nothing wrong with the car. Only that a piece of elastic was on the battery, where the wire is fastened."

"Well, that's nice and simple," Jessica said.

"But he is telling me that someone must have done it on purpose. Do you think they are after Simone?" He sounded incredulous.

"No, Marius. I think Simone was after you."

"What do you mean?"

"Well . . . I think she wanted to ride back with you and check up on you, because I was there. So she risked her long fingernails and her white dress—"

He stared thoughtfully at the ground near his feet, not saying a word. Jessica removed the yellow leaf from the car. After all those thousands of years, how could men still be so innocent?

He looked unhappy when he raised his head. Charles, too, had lost his smile. "Come," said Marius, and led them through the side door into the office wing.

They walked the length of the corridor to a large office at the end, a beautiful room with windows on three sides, and a stuffy, uninhabited feeling. The polished surface of a huge walnut desk was almost bare of work. Semiopaque curtains were drawn against the sun. Marius turned on the lights and the air conditioner.

"Is this your mother's office?" Jessica asked.

"Yes, when she is here. She used to come almost every day, but now she has not been well, perhaps because of Françoise. It is good that there are people who can take care of the business."

She was about to murmur a commiseration, when footsteps sounded briskly in the hall. A middle-aged man in a white lab coat entered the office. Following him was Mr. Augustín, who greeted Jessica effusively.

Marius introduced the man in the lab coat as a chemist. He chatted with him briefly, then unzipped his wristbag and took out the folder of pictures. Augustín reached for it, asking to see it. Marius ignored him, extracted the shot of Françoise and handed it to the chemist.

Augustín turned to Jessica. "So you have the picture of Françoise, my little friend. I wish she did give me a picture, too."

"I'm sure her family would be glad to give you one," Jessica replied.

The chemist held the picture next to a window and care-

125

fully brushed something onto it. Marius and Augustín seemed to be discussing shipments of soap. Jessica's eyes kept encountering Charles's, and they would smile at each other and then look away, embarrassed, because they could not talk. After a while Charles got up and paced the room, finally lifting a curtain on one of the side windows, to stand gazing at Simone's car. At least, Jessica reflected, Simone had no shortage of admirers.

The chemist left his window and announced that he had ascertained the missing words to be "E-l j-e-t-e."

"*Jete?*" asked Marius. "*Jete?* It throws? That makes no sense."

Jessica asked, "May I see it?"

The chemist held out the picture to her, but did not let go of it. The words were traced lightly with some kind of material that looked as though it might easily rub off. *El jete et moi. Danger! Danger! Danger!*

Frowning, she peered at it closely.

"That's not a *t*," she said, "it's an *f*. '*El jefe.*' That's Spanish for 'chief.' 'The chief and me.'"

"Chief?" Marius asked, bewildered.

"*Le chef.* The head of something. Or at least the head of part of it."

"So it tells us nothing. It does not say his name, or what he is the head of, and we cannot see from the picture who it is. You are sure you don't know this man?"

Gingerly she took the picture from the chemist, holding it by its edges. She turned it over and stared at it, trying to see something familiar in the man, while Augustín breathed beside her ear.

"Maybe we can make it bigger?" Augustín suggested. "But it is a bad picture."

"Yes, I don't know if enlarging it would help." She turned to look at him as she spoke, and saw that his face had become puckered and intense. Something in her

126

stirred at his expression, but she suppressed it. He was not the man in the picture.

She studied it again. She began to see its contours more clearly, unblurred by shadows.

"No," she said, "I really think . . ."

Marius asked eagerly, "What do you think?"

"I think—I can't believe it, but I really think it's one of those mannequins. There was one that looked something like that."

"One what? A mannequin? What is that?"

She had thought it was a French word. "You know, a dummy. Like in a store, those big dolls they display the clothes on."

Marius asked, "Are you sure?" but he was drowned by Augustín's loud laugh.

"May I see?" Augustín reached again with thick, damp fingers. She hesitated, afraid that he would destroy the chemist's work on the back, although now that they had deciphered the words, perhaps it didn't matter.

"There's nothing to see," she said. "I'm sure it's that. I thought it looked like it, but I—"

A silvery voice called from the hallway, "Monsieur Augustín, *il y a un appel téléphonique pour vous.*"

The heavy breathing quickened in her ear. He answered something about taking a message, but the voice's owner, a tall brunette, appeared in the doorway to announce that the call was from Italy and very important. Augustín excused himself and went out to the corridor.

Jessica rubbed her ear, which still felt warm from his breath. "I wonder why he was so interested."

"We are all interested," Marius said. "But why does she put herself in a picture with a doll? There must be some reason." He spoke in French to Charles.

Jessica had been tracing the edge of the photograph with her fingertip. "Maybe there's something more. It feels sort of thick, as if it's double. Did you ever notice that about Polaroids? And she did cut it to make it fit my wallet."

Marius took it from her and examined the edges. "I don't think it would open, if that is what you mean. I don't know much about this kind of picture, but it seems to be all in one piece."

"Let me try." She took it back. Marius began speaking French again, with the chemist listening, and Charles interjecting short replies. Then Marius translated for her.

"I think she uses the doll for a reason, because the picture is unimportant. She wants to tell us that it is unimportant. And I am thinking that maybe there is also some reason why she writes '*le chef*' in Spanish."

At last Jessica managed to insert her thumbnail between the front and back of the picture. With some resistance, for they had evidently been cemented together, the two sides peeled open.

"Voilà!" she exclaimed.

The three men crowded around her. Marius's theory was forgotten. The insides of both the front and back of the picture were covered with writing and strange symbols. The chemist pounced, exclaiming. One side, as they all recognized, contained a chemical formula. The other was something quite different.

"It looks like Arabic," Jessica said.

"It is," Marius agreed. "Now, where can we—"

At that moment the room shook, the windows rattled, as the world outside exploded.

14

Her first impression was the horrified look on Marius's face. He must have felt the same way when he heard his own car explode and knew Simone was in it.

Then they were all running down the corridor and through the side door to the parking lot. It seemed as though everyone in the building ran. And when they were outside, they stopped and stared, for part of the second floor in the laboratory wing had tumbled over the first.

People erupted from the main door to stand, dazed. Charles rushed toward the damage, and Jessica with him. Marius waved them back.

She heard screams. Then a second explosion.. Chunks of masonry flew into the air. Like an avalanche, the entire second-floor laboratory collapsed.

"What's happening?" she asked Charles, knowing he couldn't answer. Ahead of them, Marius disappeared into the building and a moment later brought out a white-coated chemist with a bleeding face. He shouted for someone to call the police, then helped the dazed chemist into the undamaged office wing.

When he returned, Jessica tried to reach him. He vanished into a milling crowd of employees. Charles had already gone inside to search for other injured.

She could not just stand there. She started toward the entrance. One of the men waved her back, waved them all back. She saw a large crack in one of the standing walls. A siren shrilled in the distance.

Mr. Augustín came out of the office door, looked around, and hurried toward her.

"What has happened?"

"The laboratory blew up," she said.

"Blew up? How can that be?"

"I don't know, Monsieur Augustín. I doubt if anybody knows yet."

"What did you learn about the picture? Who has the picture of my little Françoise?"

"Does it matter, for God's sake?" she asked impatiently.

He bustled over to the chemist who had been with them in Mme. Lannier's office. She saw him speak, and the chemist shake his head. She honestly could not remember who had the picture when the explosion occurred.

A police car tore into the parking lot. More sirens screamed. Emergency vehicles came from everywhere, fire trucks and ambulances. The air was heavy with the smell of smoke and perfume. Marius paused beside her as the firemen began an organized entry into the building.

"What happened?" she asked. "Perfume isn't explosive, is it? A bomb?"

"It was from the laboratory of Henri," he replied sharply. "It was not the perfume."

"Was he here?"

"They have not seen him." He left her and went back to help the firemen.

She rested against one of the cars. It was a safe place, where she would not be in the way.

He had sounded annoyed with her. Why? Because nothing had happened before she came?

But there had been Françoise. And even Bernard Martin, whose death was probably not connected, but it might have been.

Bernard Martin. He had managed the factory. And

130

Weyland worked here, in a laboratory that was now destroyed.

She could not think. Not in this smoke and confusion.

Two men carried a stretcher from the building. On it was a sheet-covered figure. She turned away. If the figure was dead, she did not want to know it.

After a while, Marius came out through the main door. His hands and arms were blackened, his shirt smudged, and he looked exhausted.

She wove her way toward him among the people and vehicles. "Marius, is it bad?"

He ran a hand through his hair, dirtying that, too. "Certainly it is bad. What do you think?"

"I mean, were many people hurt?"

"Yes. Many were hurt, some very badly. So far, thank God, we have found no one killed."

"I'm glad about that much." She moved out of the way as Charles came over to his friend, put an arm around him and patted his shoulder.

"Don't blame yourself," Charles seemed to be saying. She caught the name "Henri." Something Henri had been doing. *Il a fait.* Or making.

Henri . . . Explosives . . .

Henri . . . *"Mon ami."*

Then Charles asked, "Is it possible to leave now? Simone will be waiting for us."

"You may leave," Marius told him wearily. "Take Zhessica with you, please. I cannot go yet."

"Please," Charles said to her in English, and led the way across the parking lot. He held open the passenger door of Simone's car and bowed politely for her to enter.

It was a long drive back to Nice. In order to make the trip more bearable for both of them, she overcame her inhibitions as best she could and dusted off her awkward French.

Charles was ecstatic. Nothing, it seemed, could dampen his spirits for long. He enjoyed her French, corrected her tactfully, and learned to speak slowly so that she could understand. She told him about her trip, about seeing Henri on the train, and explained where she intended to go next. She did not tell him about the invasion of her room, or her encounter with Henri in his car. Those were beyond her capabilities.

When they reached Nice, Charles invited her to dinner, despite her smudged yellow slacks and his own dirty hands. They could wash in the restaurant lavatory, he said.

She asked, "What about Simone?" He looked at his watch and shrugged. She was not sure what he answered, but had the impression that it was the wrong hour to visit Simone, or that there was still plenty of time, although earlier he had been so eager.

They went to a restaurant near the Cimiez section, far from her usual territory. It was a leisurely dinner of bouillabaisse, the first she had had on the Riviera.

"Marseilles," he told her enthusiastically, "is the best place to eat bouillabaisse."

She replied that in a few days she would be there, which launched him into a catalog of the things she should see and do.

Only when they were finished did he begin to show that he was in a hurry. He called loudly for *l'addition,* and then drove her straight to her hotel. When they arrived at its entrance, he jumped from the car and opened the door for her.

"Good night, Charles, and thank you for everything." After he had gotten back into the car, she leaned on the window and added, "Please give my regards to Simone."

Oh, definitely he would. *"Merci et bonne nuit!"* With a flourish of his hand, he was off.

She hurried into the hotel, still smiling to herself from the contagion of his own good humor. As she started toward the elevator at the rear of the lobby, someone rose from a chair behind a large pillar and blocked her way.

A light shone in back of him. Her eyes, still unaccustomed to the interior, saw his face only dimly, but could not miss the powerful shoulders and wide head.

He peered around the pillar as a laughing group came in through the hotel entrance. Quickly he pushed her into the elevator and pressed the button. Fifth floor. So he already knew her room.

Despite the elegance of the hotel, the elevator was old and slow. It jerked its way upward and stopped on the second floor. There was a pause before the door opened. He murmured something, drawing her attention to the pocket of his dark jacket. Briefly she glimpsed a small gun, with his hand on it, ready to pull the trigger.

The door opened to disclose two middle-aged couples speaking English. Weyland mouthed the word "Up," and pointed. One of the women smiled and went on talking, and the door closed.

"What do you want from me?" Jessica asked.

"We will discuss that when we get to your room," he replied.

"You wouldn't really fire that gun in a crowded hotel."

"Do you want to take a chance?"

The door opened at the fifth floor and he waved her to precede him. She looked down a long expanse of carpeted hallway and closed doors. No one was in sight. He placed his hand in the middle of her back and guided her gently to her room.

"You will please to unlock the door?" His voice was as smooth as ever, his manner almost caressing.

As soon as they were inside, he double-locked and chained the door.

"Please tell me what you want," she said again. "I tried to take your advice about leaving Nice, but I couldn't change my reservation. I'm leaving Sunday."

"Yes, of course," he responded indifferently. She was not sure he had heard her.

133

She asked, "Do you know what happened at Grasse this afternoon?"

"Yes, I know. It was on the radio." He checked the bathroom, the balcony, the wardrobe. The gun was out of his pocket now and aimed vaguely in her direction. The drapes were open and the room still hot from the afternoon sunshine. All that lovely glass wall, and it only faced the sea.

He said, "Why don't you make yourself comfortable?"

"How can I?"

"Sit down." It was an invitation rather than an order. He gestured to the only upholstered chair. For himself, he pulled out the wooden straight-backed chair from the desk. Just as Marius had done.

"Now," he said, when they were seated across the glass-topped table from each other, "I want you to tell me everything you can."

"About what?"

She wondered if he knew she had continued to see Marius. Undoubtedly he did. He even knew she had moved to this hotel.

"About," he said, "our friend Françoise."

"I think probably you know more about her than I do."

"That is not what I asked. I asked what *you* know."

He looked at her hands, her whitened fingers gripping the seat of the chair. "Why don't you relax a little bit? We have very much time."

"How much? And what happens then?"

He settled back himself, the gun dangling loosely from his fingers. "We will know when it is the right moment. Now tell me. You know when I was there to see Françoise at your university. After that, did she give you anything to keep? Did she tell you anything to do?"

So he was the one, all along.

"What—" She played for time, although he had said there was plenty. "What sort of thing?"

134

"Ah, I see that you understand me. Yes, you are nervous now."

Then there was nothing he didn't know. All he wanted was that she admit it. She raised her chin slightly and replied, "It was only a picture."

"A picture. That is good." He did not seem in the least surprised. "Did she tell you anything about the picture? Anything to do with it?"

"No, just keep it. Take it to Nice."

He leaned forward eagerly. The sudden motion made her wince.

"Don't be afraid, young lady," he said. "Only give me the picture. It is true we are a little late with this, other arrangements have already been made. But you were supposed to, how do you say, make it accessible. Someone was to get it from you. I thought she would tell you."

"She didn't. And I—don't have it."

"You—have not—it?" He slapped his forehead. "All this—But she promised me."

"Well, you know, she was killed," Jessica pointed out. "Maybe she never had a chance to tell me."

"She gave you the picture, didn't she?"

"Yes, but . . ."

"And you came without it."

So he didn't even know she had brought it to Europe. She began to feel a glimmer of hope. If he knew what she had done with it, he might kill her.

"I came as a tourist," she explained. "That's all, just a tourist. She knew I was planning to come here, and—"

"*Yes,* she knew you were coming, that is the point. That is why she gave you this message. You were a courier, my dear lady, an unwitting courier, but it seems you did not receive your instructions. Oh, mon Dieu, mon Dieu."

Was all this arranged, then? It was *for* Françoise?

"Why is it important?" she wanted to know.

"It is very important. You do not need to know why."

"If Françoise sent it, then why didn't you just ask me for it? Why did you have to search my room, and climb on my balcony, and have me attacked on the street?"

"Eh? Who did all these things? Who attacked you on the street?"

"I thought they were muggers. They tried to grab my purse. It's ridiculous. If I was supposed to bring it to you, why couldn't you just ask? *I* didn't know what you wanted."

He sat dejectedly in the wooden chair. The only thing still alert was the hand that held the gun.

"I didn't know what I wanted, either," he said. "Only a message. I did not know in what form it would come. I asked, and you said you had nothing. So I had to be careful. You might have been—" He stopped, his eyes narrowing.

"Might have been what?"

"We have," he began with a sigh, "an enemy who sabotages our whole operation. Françoise was to find out who is this enemy, since the contact was hers, and send the information to me. A telephone call or a letter might be stopped. So she would send a message with you, but they try to stop me from getting it. And now you didn't bring it. Ah well, it is too late, but we could still disable this enemy if we know who it is. Tell me, what was the picture? Was it a man? Old? Young?"

"It wasn't anything." She did not know how to tell him. "It was only Françoise and a—one of those dummies they use in stores, with the clothes on."

His muscular face grew taut and his eyes hawklike. "*What*? Tell me the truth!"

"That is the truth. I didn't know at first. We—I think she was trying to show that the picture was not important."

"Not important? What do you mean?"

"That's what I mean. That whatever you were expecting—it wasn't in the picture."

136

"There was nothing else? No message?"

It didn't matter, she told herself. Françoise was dead. Nothing could touch her now. He claimed to be her friend and ally, but there he was, pointing a gun at Jessica.

He did not like her hesitation. "What else? Tell me the rest."

She looked down at her hands, to keep her eyes away from his face and the gun.

"But that's what's so strange. On the back she wrote *El jefe et moi.*"

She glanced at him to see whether he understood. "That's Spanish for 'the chief.' *El jefe et moi,* and underneath, *Danger! Danger! Danger!,* and then she rubbed it all out. We—"

She had almost given away the fact that Marius had seen it. Then he would know she had lied.

"I had to rub a pencil over it to be able to read it," she went on. "And that made me think the picture was more than just a keepsake, so I looked inside. It was a Polaroid, you can peel them open."

"Wait a minute, what does she say? In Spanish? And why rub it out?"

"I didn't understand that, either," Jessica replied, glad of the reprieve. She regretted that she had told him so much, and betrayed her lack of innocence regarding the picture.

And again she remembered that he was Françoise's friend and she had been sent to help him.

He muttered, "In Spanish. It might mean someone who is Spanish, yes? Or someone . . ." And then he appeared to register what she had just said. "There was something inside the picture?"

"Yes, but I don't know why she was sending it to you. I'd have thought you knew all about it. There was some Arabic writing on one side, which of course I couldn't read, and a chemical formula—"

She stopped, horrified, as he rose from the chair. He seemed almost to have forgotten the gun, and brandished it carelessly close to her eyes.

"What do you say?"

She shook her head, pleading with him, but could not speak. He was going to kill her. Blow her face away.

Finally she managed, "I thought you'd want to know. Your message—"

He sat down again heavily, his head in his hand, the gun resting loosely on his knee. She might have gotten up, but she was paralyzed. And he would be quick.

"Not that. Not that," he said in despair. "If that is what she sent, it was for someone else, not for me."

His hands tightened, and she drew back, fearing the trigger.

"She has *betrayed* me," he choked. "Betrayed . . . oh, God, God, God!"

15

She waited, not daring to move. In a way, she almost pitied him; his anguish was sincere. But what would happen when the shock receded? Françoise was not there to kill.

After a while he sat down and quietly watched her. Then he asked, "That is the truth, what you tell me?"

"I wouldn't make it up," she answered. He wanted to talk. It was better for her, if she could keep him talking. She said, "The chemical formula. Was it yours?"

"Mine, yes. An explosive that I invented." He spoke shortly. The velvet voice had gone. "She asked me for the formula. It should be safe, she said, if something happens to me. To me." He tapped himself on the chest.

Jessica said, "Now it's blown up at the factory, hurt a lot of people and maybe killed some. And there was the bomb in Marius's car."

He raised his hands and let them fall, but he still held the gun.

"That was not from me. I never tried to hurt Marius, although God knows I did not want him to find out what we are doing. It was the others, who don't want anybody to know about *them,* who take our powder and use it against us everywhere. And she—"

"That powder," Jessica said. "You were making it in your laboratory at Grasse, weren't you? Did you ever stop to think about the other people there?"

"It is impossible. The powder I invented was especially stable. That was one advantage of it. It could be shipped, transported through heat—"

"Through hot deserts?"

"Yes. And only a little bit is needed. And it cannot be discovered by the dogs that are trained to find the explosives."

"But it did blow up at Grasse."

"That was not my powder. There was nothing of my powder in the laboratory."

"Then what happened?"

"I have said they use it against us. They are trying to destroy our operation. To destroy me. Maybe they hoped I would be there and they could kill me. It was probably a timed device, or remote control. And you see, if it goes from my laboratory, that is to put the blame on me, as they do everywhere else." He wiped his hand across his face.

She said, "In Saudi Arabia, do you mean? The pipelines?"

His hand paused in midwipe. He stared at her.

"You were making that powder to ship to Yemen, weren't you?" she asked.

He continued to stare. Then he said, "I asked her to help me. Françoise. I wanted to send it to the rebels. There was no one to give them any help. They did not even have the guns. Françoise said to ship them guns, but me I played around with my formula and this would be better. We can ship it as something else, maybe the bath powder, and no one will know. So I asked her to arrange the shipping. Me, I have not such contacts."

So that was the exporting business. And Françoise had gone to Marius for help, and he had introduced her to Claude Augustín.

But obviously that had not worked out.

"What happened?" she asked, to make him talk again.

"What happened?" He sounded dazed. "They did find out. That is what happened. Not the French authorities, but our enemy, and they divert our shipments to their own guerrillas. They would try to destroy not only our rebels, but the Saudi Arabia as it is, and make a Communist government. I do not necessarily believe in kings, but the Communists, I spit on them."

"Then why," she said again, "the pipelines?"

"They do it. They. And they say it is the rebels, to make everyone fight against the rebels."

She nodded, to show her understanding. It had certainly worked as propaganda. Even the media had fallen for it.

"At first," he said, "we did not know what is happening. Then one of our people finds out, and we must discover who is doing this. So I went to *her.*" He gave a slight toss of the head, a gesture that showed his contempt. "Probably she was the one."

"You didn't have any idea?"

"How could I? She pretended to be my friend. Even more than a friend. I thought she was a little girl, only twenty-three years old, and so innocent. I thought I knew all about these things, but it is the other way around. *I* am the one who is innocent. I know nothing, and she—"

"It might not have been that way," Jessica said. "They might have forced her. All during the spring she seemed very nervous and frightened about something."

"About the Bernard Martin."

"Why?"

"Why? Because it is against the law to kill people."

"Do you mean—? Not Françoise!"

"She said it was because he finds out what we are doing. Now I don't know. Maybe they ordered her to do it, but that is why she went to the United States and would not come back."

She felt as though she had turned to jelly, hearing him

141

say those things about Françoise. Yet somehow she knew he was speaking the truth.

"But she really was frightened," Jessica said. "Maybe they held that over her, if she did it. It could work, you know. That's the sort of thing they do."

"Young lady, I have had more experience of them than you have."

He looked at her suddenly, sharply, probably suspecting her, too. She dared not say anything.

Françoise. . . . How was it possible? So many things had happened recently that she found hard to believe, but this?

"So," he continued, "I went to her to find out the name of her contact, so we can know who has betrayed us. She says she can't tell me right away. She knows only the nickname. So she will find out and send me. That is what she was supposed to give you." He pointed toward Jessica with the gun. "Instead she asks me for the formula. So it will be safe, she says. Safe." Again the disdainful head toss. "And also for the names of my contacts in Al Hudayda and San'a. So I write it out for her. I write in Arabic, but she copies it. For *them.*"

She was silent, still trying to grasp it all. On the surface she could accept what he said, even about Bernard Martin, because of the way he said it, but she needed time to absorb the whole thing and make it more than just words.

And she did not know whether she had any time.

"What are you going to do now?" she asked.

"What I am going to do? I am going to wait."

"For what? I told you I don't have the picture."

He sat back in his chair, rocking it on two legs, the gun still pointed at her. Despite the fact that his quarrel was not with her, he could use the gun if he felt cornered, or angry enough, or if she tried to get away.

His gaze wandered around the room and finally settled again on her.

142

"Why don't you go to sleep?" he asked. "It will be a long night."

She hid her dismay at this remark and answered calmly, "No longer than most nights, I should imagine, at this time of year."

He replied with equal serenity, "It depends upon what one is doing. If one is sleeping, it passes quickly. There is no need for you to sit up."

Her calm vanished and she demanded, "How long are you going to stay here, anyway?"

"As long as I must."

"Until *what*? Look, I haven't got the picture, and there's no way I can get it in the near future, so what is this going to accomplish?"

He watched her for a moment before he answered.

"Two things. The first is, you will not be able to talk to anyone and give us more danger than we already have. And second, with the explosion in the factory, and Marius knowing my background, it is quite possible that he can guess what I have been doing. But if you are with me, I think he will not try to stop us."

"Stop you—from what?"

"From what we do next. And that you will find out only when it is time."

So he had got her. But why her? He must still have wanted the picture, probably more than ever, now that he knew it contained his own precious secrets. And yet he believed she hadn't brought it.

She wondered why Françoise had sent it after all, the nonpicture with that irrelevant inscription on the back.

But, of course—in case Weyland, who was expecting a message himself, got hold of it first. It would keep him happily unsuspicious of what was inside.

She dreaded having to sit there and face him. But she did not want the passivity of sleeping. It would somehow imply an acceptance of her situation.

Now that he had gone this far, he would scarcely dare leave her alive. Again she took stock of the room, trying to figure a way out.

The balcony. It was right there beside her, but how could she ever manage it? Even if she could swing up to the roof, as her night visitor had evidently done, Weyland would be right behind her.

Out the door, if he started to doze. But she would have to go around the bed, and he was in the way. She could roll across it, but that would make just enough disturbance to wake him.

All this was predicated on the possibility that he might sleep, and so far he showed no signs of it.

The sudden shrilling of the telephone made her jump. She looked over at it, on the far side of the bed, and then at Weyland. It rang again.

"Answer it," he said. "Behave as you always would." He made room for her to get around the bed, and followed her with the gun.

Now, at least, she was nearer the door, but he was right with her. She picked up the phone.

It was Marius. "Ah, Zhessica, I almost began to think you were not there. I was worried. How is everything?"

"Just—fine." She could hear Weyland shifting his feet only a short distance away.

"I have come from Grasse, just now," Marius continued. "The police, they think it must have been a bomb. They have found pieces of metal. Do you know that no one was killed, but some were badly hurt. The explosion was in the laboratory of Henri, and that was empty. I do not know all what is happening, Zhessica, but now we have the police both in Nice and in Grasse to look for who is doing this."

She tried to think of something to say, some way to alert him.

But anything that would be significant to Marius, who

144

was all unsuspecting, Weyland would be sure to pick up.

"Zhessica, are you still there? Are you all right?"

"I'm okay. I'm glad—about Grasse. That no one was killed. And thank you for the day. Up until then, it was a lovely trip."

"Yes," he said, "I am sorry that you were there when it happened. I am sorry, in fact, that it happened. But I wanted to be sure that Charles got you back to your hotel all right, and that you had no trouble."

"Trouble?" she repeated. It came out more sharply than she had intended. She heard Weyland catch his breath.

Marius explained, "I had a little trouble myself, coming back. There was a car that followed me, driving very fast. I feel it tried to push me off the road, but I knew another way that was confusing to this driver. I think maybe we have come close enough to them so that now we are dangerous. That is why I want to be sure that you are all right."

"At least you got away," Jessica said. She tried to put a slight emphasis on the "you." Weyland's hand clamped around her wrist.

"Yes, it was lucky," Marius replied. "You are probably very tired, Zhessica, so good-night."

When she hung up the phone, Weyland asked, "That was Marius?"

"Yes. Someone chased his car back from Grasse and tried to force him off the road."

"So they think he has the picture. And you did bring it to France?"

"It wasn't that," she said, not meeting his eyes, fearful that her face would betray her. "He thinks it's because he's been getting too suspicious."

"Suspicious of whom?"

"He didn't say." She sat down again in her orange chair and stared sullenly at the floor.

145

"What are you going to do with me?" she asked again.

"You will find out tomorrow," he replied. "In the meantime, as I have already said, why don't you sleep?"

He only wanted to make her unconscious so that he could relax a little, too.

"I'll tell you what I want," she said. "I would like to go to the bathroom, and I would like to do it alone."

He appeared confused. "To take a bath?"

"No." She realized that "bathroom" was a euphemism bewildering to Europeans, and that she would have to be more straightforward. *"Toilette."*

"Ah, but of course." He stood up from his chair.

"It's near the door. Will you let me go in alone?"

At first she was afraid he would not, for he went with her and checked the room to see that there was no egress. After assuring himself that it was an inside bathroom without a window, and had only a vent too small to crawl through, he withdrew.

She was left alone, feeling self-conscious because of the thin walls. She turned on a water faucet for sound camouflage and studied the room as Weyland had done. There was certainly no way out. She considered banging an SOS on one of the pipes. But he would hear it—and would be quicker than anyone else to understand its meaning.

Even before she opened the door, she heard his voice. He had carried the telephone, on its long wire, across the narrow entryway, so he could watch her when she came out of the bathroom. He was speaking in a language she did not recognize. Arabic? With the gun still in his hand, he waved her back to her chair. When his call was finished, he rejoined her.

"Is this going to go on all night?" she asked. "Just sitting here and staring at each other?"

He answered wearily, "I have repeatedly suggested that you may sleep. It would certainly be less boring than, as you say, sitting and staring at each other."

146

"I hardly need to point out," she said, "that these are not optimum conditions for sleeping. In the first place, I don't like people watching me when I sleep, and in the second place, I don't like guns."

"Maybe, when you are tired enough . . ."

And so they remained for another half hour, until there was a knock at the door.

She started up hopefully. Weyland stopped her with his eyes as he went to the door and spoke through it. The answer, in the same language he had used on the telephone, made her realize that this was help for him, not for her.

He unlocked and unchained the door, and admitted a dark, slender young man with black, curly hair. The newcomer looked her over, seeming to absorb all the details in one brief inspection. The two men conferred in the same slightly guttural language. Arabic, she was sure of it now. They both looked at her and she felt like something on display. She was their prisoner, they were talking about her, and she could not understand them.

Then Weyland said to her, "This is my friend Fayez. He is here to keep us company, to make the night a little bit shorter."

She wondered what he meant by that.

"Pleased to meet you, I'm sure," she told Fayez. He nodded, but her sarcasm was lost on him. He did not, it seemed, understand English.

The two men settled down, Weyland in his chair, which he had pulled back a little way so that he could talk with Fayez, who leaned against the wall. Jessica glanced at her travel clock, ticking on the table beside the bed. A lot of good that protective alarm had done her in the end. A lump of misery rose in her throat. Would she live to see her father again, who had so lovingly tried to keep his daughter safe with that little gift? She had not even begun her trip.

She pressed her lips together to keep her feelings from showing. After a while the lump melted away.

"You know," she told Weyland, "I never asked to be involved in any of this. It's hardly my fault that Françoise picked me as a courier, or that she betrayed you. And I didn't know what you wanted, chasing me around like that. I really had no idea."

"I chased you?" he asked in mock surprise. "It seems to me that I was running from you, from the first shock of our meeting in Gare de Lyon. I never expected to see you, or for you to see me. But after you saw me, I thought I might as well make the contact myself."

"So you had somebody run me down with a motorcycle."

"No, no." He held up his hand. "You blame me for everything. I was on my way to see you when the motorcycle happened. I caught you from falling, but then you seemed afraid of me. There must be a reason, yes? And maybe you are that reason. Maybe you know you are my enemy. That is how I saw it."

"There was a reason," she said. "I thought you killed Françoise, and you were going to kill me. And now look— I was right to be afraid of you. I can just imagine how this is going to end. And all because I tried to be friends with someone . . . I wish I'd never heard of the bitch."

"So do I, dear lady, so do I." He shook his head sadly. "And if you know how this is going to end, you know more than I do. I told you she has betrayed the names of my friends at home. This I know. I write in Arabic because I don't know how to spell the names in French. It was the only thing I gave her in Arabic, and she must have copied it. I only hope you left that picture in a very safe place."

"It's safer than I am," she retorted, "and I don't give a damn about your troubles. I'm not doing anything to you, you're doing it to me. All I wanted was a nice trip to Europe. I looked forward to it all year."

Again she had to bite her lip, but could not stop the tears that filled her eyes. She pressed her hands to her face, and through the ensuing darkness, heard them talking again. Then Weyland took her arm. She tried to pull away.

"It is best that you sleep," he told her firmly. "Here is your bed. We will turn off the light so it will be easier for you."

There must be some way out of this, she thought, too spent to resist as he helped her onto the bed. He tried to lift the covers over her, but she slapped his hand away. She had to maintain a little control, however ludicrous. Lying on top of the bed instead of in it made her feel a degree less vulnerable.

They turned out the light, as they had promised. Some city glow came in through the windows. It outlined the two men, dark shapes in the gray room.

She realized that she was still wearing her shoes. She made no move to take them off. Far away she heard voices, a radio playing symphonic music. She heard someone laugh. For everyone else in Nice, it was a normal Thursday night. And on Sunday, she should have been leaving for Marseilles.

16

She had not expected to sleep, but when she woke and saw that it was daylight, she realized she had.

She woke without a moment's confusion, remembering at once where she was and what had happened, and she looked for the two men. Weyland had taken the orange chair, and the younger Fayez had inherited the wooden one. They glanced at her when they heard her stirring to wakefulness, and then turned politely away.

According to the clock, it was already seven. A warm, fresh breeze blew softly in through her balcony door.

Maybe Steve will call, she thought hopefully, and then remembered that he did not know she had changed her hotel.

And Marius . . . even if she could manage to hint something, Marius, because of the language difference, would probably not understand.

In any case, it was still early, and the telephone remained silent. She closed her eyes again, so that she would not have to look at the men, but she did not sleep. No doubt they had hung the Do Not Disturb sign on the door. It would be hours before anyone took notice of this room and its occupants. But eventually, she knew from experience, the maids would feel that they had to get in here. Thank God it was a hotel and not some country hideaway. At least there were people around, even though they might have been miles away, for all the chance she had of reaching them.

After a while her companions began to show signs of activity. They took turns in the bathroom, then told her she could go in, if she wanted to.

"I don't want to," she said angrily, unwilling to oblige, and feeling even more self-conscious, now that there were two of them.

"You had better do it," Weyland told her. "It might be difficult later on."

So they were going somewhere. How would they get her out of the hotel without anyone noticing that she was being coerced? Even if she broke away, they could hardly shoot her in a hotel lobby.

"It must be a terribly worthy destination," she ventured, "since you waited here all night when you probably have more important things to do."

"We wait for the morning," Weyland explained, not in the least disturbed by her sarcasm or curiosity, "because it is a busy time downstairs. At night we would be noticed."

So that was the reason. They had thought of everything. She hadn't a chance. Once more she settled into a lethargy of hopelessness, to wait.

When they did leave, shortly before nine, Weyland, as the more respectable-looking of the two in his business suit, walked beside her, holding tightly to her arm. Fayez, just behind them, carried the gun beneath a jacket draped over his hand.

Weyland had made her wear sunglasses. In the dimness of the lobby when they first got off the elevator, she could barely see. Ahead of her the entrance blazed in morning sunlight, and all around her were the shapes of people, bright sports clothes, mounds of luggage. A tour group was getting ready to leave: an excellent cover.

They emerged onto the sidewalk and she felt the warmth of the day. A tour bus waited at curbside, its engine roaring for the sake of the air conditioning. Weyland marched her past it into the morning bustle of the sidewalk.

She had not done anything, not tried to break away, or cry out. He must have guessed she would be passive. Was it a culturized inhibition, a refusal to make a scene? Or was it the gun? She could not be sure. In any case, she despised herself. There was no advantage in such submissiveness. It would scarcely help her in the end.

Halfway down the block, a car stood waiting for them. She did not notice it until Weyland opened the back door and gently pushed her inside. He got in after her, and Fayez climbed into the front seat beside the driver, who was nothing but a head of dark wavy hair and, in the mirror, a glimpse of sunglasses.

It was Weyland's car, she recognized it. Probably the back door had a remote control lock, just like the front. Hardly necessary, for Fayez turned around to pass the gun back to Weyland as the car started off into a stream of rush-hour traffic.

She had gone this way with Marius. Only yesterday?

She had gone to that beach over there with Steve. It seemed so long ago, those innocent days with Steve. Why hadn't he stayed in Nice and kept her safe?

This was the road to Grasse. She remembered it.

But they did not stay on the road to Grasse. Sometime later, they switched to another. To Vence? His flat in Vence? Someone would see them there. Marius would guess where she was.

But he did not even know she was with Weyland. If he tried to call her, he would only think she had gone out shopping, or to the beach.

And why would he try to call her? He had called last night to see if she had gotten back safely. There was no further reason to call. He would be busy at his own office today (Friday?) or possibly at the factory. There was much to do there, investigation and rebuilding.

She leaned back and closed her eyes. All this was speculation. Whatever happened would happen. She had been deprived of her autonomy and, as she could not act, she might as well not think.

She gazed out of the window, apathetically watching the scenery that had once so captivated her. Even now she recognized its beauty, but was no longer interested. She felt only dull despair.

The olive trees, the flower farms. They were not going to Vence, they were somewhere in the mountains beyond it. As they rounded a bend, she saw on her right a deep wild gorge. Perhaps the Loup Valley. She could not tell. He was driving too fast for this road. They might end up in a fiery crash at the bottom of the gorge.

The men had been silent for the most part during the trip, only now and then exchanging a few remarks in Arabic. Now she sensed a tension, an alertness. They rounded another bend and the gorge was lost from sight. The car slowed and made a sharp turn onto a rutted dirt road that cut through the remnants of a stone wall, or part of a foundation. Olive trees rustled in a hot breeze.

They bounced along the road for a few yards and then stopped. The car was so low that she could not at first see where they were. The men began to pile out. The driver, who was closest to her door, opened it and helped her onto the dry ground with a gentle chivalry that seemed oddly misplaced under such circumstances. The sunglasses hid his eyes, but he had a high-bridged nose and a full mouth. Like Fayez, he appeared younger than Weyland, who was evidently their leader.

Now she noticed a stone farmhouse, like the ones near the factory at Grasse. The earth around it had gone to dry, wild grasses. It looked only semi-inhabited, and that impression was confirmed when Weyland opened the door and directed her inside. There was furniture, but no lived-in feeling. No curtains or knickknacks, and

153

only a bare mattress on the bed in the room to which they led her.

A chest of drawers stood in a corner, and on each of two walls was a narrow window. Narrow to keep out the blazing sunshine, she supposed. The room was cool, dim, and stuffy.

Fayez and the driver threw her down on the bed. She struggled, but rape was not in their minds. They tied her hands together, then her feet, and pulled a soft gag across her mouth, carefully adjusting it so she could breathe. What if I had a cold, she wondered, and in a sudden panic of claustrophobia, shook her head to try to loosen the gag. They readjusted it and left the room, looking back at her once as they closed the door. She heard a key turn. How ridiculous. As if she could even get up off the bed with her feet tied.

She wanted to call out, to scream. There would be no one to hear her except the three men, and they had gagged her, not wanting to be plagued with her noise. She must not cry. That would make her nose run, and then she would suffocate.

They wouldn't leave her here forever. Or perhaps that would be an easy solution. Evidently they did not intend to kill her. If they had, they could have done it back at the hotel, or dumped her body by the roadside and saved themselves this trouble.

What, then? What would they do with her?

He had said something about Marius . . . so that Marius would let them go. She had not absorbed it then—that she was a hostage.

But what would Marius care?

What if nobody cared?

Fayez and his friend had opened the windows, she noticed, as soft moving air touched her face. She had not seen them do it.

Mentally she measured the windows. Extremely narrow.

154

Probably she would not be able to get her shoulders through, even if she were not tied.

From where she lay on the bed, she could see nothing but green leaves. She wondered what else was out there.

Far in the distance, through the thick walls, she heard the sound of heavy objects scraping and being rolled. Barrels? Kegs? And then a coldness washed over her. This must be where they stored the explosives. No longer in bath-powder containers. Huge quantities. They were moving it, taking it away.

She looked around the room at the bare whitewashed walls. There was nothing but the chest of drawers, this wooden bedstead, and two slender windows. And the locked door.

She struggled, trying to free her hands. The rope cut into her wrists. Something to saw it with . . . Again she examined her surroundings. Outside the windows, the house was rough stone. In here, nothing but smooth walls.

If she could only get up and somehow hop across the room. Maybe there was something in the chest.

I'll bet it's empty, she thought. Like the house.

If she started to hop, and fell, she might not be able to stand up again.

More scraping and rolling. How many barrels? How could he make so much powder without anyone knowing?

He had only developed it in the lab. Perhaps manufactured it here.

How did I get into all this? she wondered.

Françoise, deciding to go to college. A good, innocent cover, but in the end it hadn't helped. Who had killed her? Weyland? But he hadn't known of her betrayal until last night.

She sat on the edge of the bed, looking for some spot in the room, some rough place. There had to be something.

But there wasn't. Not anything.

The chest. It had to have something in it. You wouldn't just keep an empty chest.

She rose to her feet. She tried hopping, and nearly lost her balance. A better way, she discovered, was to move by twisting her feet from side to side. It swung her hips back and forth. She felt ridiculous, but no one could see her.

At last she reached the chest. She had to turn her back to it and feel for the drawer pulls. She could not spread her arms enough to grasp both sides at once, and when the drawer was pulled crookedly, it stuck. She eased it out bit by bit, alternately one side and then the other. It had some weight to it. Not much, but some. It was not empty.

Finally she had pulled it out far enough so that she could see inside.

It contained a folded blue blanket.

She must not give up. Below her she heard their voices, and more scraping sounds. They were in a cellar of some kind. What if they came in and found her like this, trying to get away? They would bind her more tightly, tie her to the bed.

And then she realized what she had been staring at: the door was recessed and, where the wall turned a corner to form the recess, some of the smooth plaster had been chipped. At that corner, there was a six-inch strip of rough stone.

But higher than her hands. It was almost on a level with her chest, and her hands were tied in back. Still, she had to try it.

Again she began to twist across the floor. The strain of her awkward position began to tell on her. Her body swung too far and her knees buckled. She barely caught herself by counterbalancing.

Nearly there. But it was not enough. She stood with her back to the rough place and strained her arms upward, feeling with her fingers. Nothing. She held her breath. A little higher. Higher. She could not reach. It was impossible.

She forced herself—another centimeter. She felt that she would die.

And then she touched it. Barely. She could never stay in

that position long enough to scrape her ropes against the corner, much less scrape them until they were sawed through.

She reached again, pushing with everything that was in her, and then again, still harder. Desperation gave her more stamina than she would have imagined she had. Still, she had to do it in small spurts.

The rolling sound had stopped. She heard their voices, raised.

Sweat poured down her back and legs. It would take forever. The effort of raising her arms so high in back made her sick. Her head grew light with fatigue, with hunger. She had not eaten since last night.

Even if she could cut through the rope, the door was locked.

They were outside now, in front of the house, shouting and arguing. How could they? This must have been important to them.

The voices faded and an engine roared. She was soaked with sweat. Her muscles ached, her head spun.

The engine roared but did not go anywhere. It might have been a generator, but it sounded like a truck.

Something popped against her wrist. She tried to pull her hands apart. The rope held fast.

She had not really believed she could do it. It was impossible, a crazy idea.

But she must keep trying. She forced her arms up once more. Her head fell forward. Her eyes were closed. It helped, for some reason, to close her eyes.

She opened them in a last effort to stay conscious. The steady roar might have been a truck, or her head. Her hands felt easier now, but the walls rocked and darkened. She felt herself falling. She was barely aware when, with a slap, the cold floor hit her face.

17

For the third time, the hotel switchboard told him she was not there.

"But she must be there," he insisted. "Where would she go? It's still early." It was not so early now, but he had started calling at half-past nine. He added, "This is important."

"I'm sorry," the operator told him patiently, "but there is no answer."

"Can you send someone to her room?"

"No, I can't do that."

He dropped the receiver into place. It was no use getting angry with the operator, she had her job and her rules to follow. But he was angry all the same. Here was a crisis, and that irritating woman remained so calm.

"Is something wrong, Monsieur Lannier?" his secretary asked, seeing him glower at the telephone.

"The police," he said, not explaining. He needed Jessica to meet with the police and tell them what she knew of Henri. He was worried, too, when he could not reach her. He had not thought Henri was vicious, but those bombs . . .

"I will need a car," he told the girl. "Call a rental agency. Nothing expensive, but I can't go around all the time in taxis."

"You're leaving?" she asked in surprise. "But you've hardly been here all week."

He shrugged. It could not be helped. This week was not an ordinary one, certainly, and with that explosion in the factory . . .

The girl started to dial the rental agency. "Nothing expensive," Marius reminded her. It was silly to waste money on unimportant things. He slipped on his suit jacket, despite the heat, and went out to pick up the car.

He drove first to the Hôtel Côte d'Azur. He had to park around the corner, and even then it wasn't legal, but he hadn't time to drive around endlessly.

He walked to the hotel and took the elevator up to her room. There he found the door ajar and a maid making up the bed.

"She's not here?" Marius asked. It was almost noon. Why so late with the bed?

The maid, an Italian, explained in voluble and broken French, "No, you see, there was the sign on the door not to disturb her, but we have to clean the room, so after some time they telephoned from downstairs, and no one answered."

Marius checked the outside of the door. Anyone could forget to remove the sign. It meant nothing. Her suitcase lay on a folding rack next to the desk, or dressing table, or whatever it was. The suitcase was zipped closed. On a hunch, he opened it.

"Monsieur!" exclaimed the maid.

"It's all right," he told her calmly, "I'm a friend of the young woman's." Not that that would reassure the maid, but his hunch had been correct. Her pocketbook was inside. He knew she kept it there when she was in the room, and she would not have gone out without it. Not if she had left of her own volition.

"Have you finished with the bed?" he asked. "Then we will go together. And you, madame, will come downstairs with me, to assure yourself that I am not a thief. You see, she left this." He drew out the pocketbook and reclosed the suitcase. "I know she didn't mean to leave it. We will take it downstairs and ask them at the desk to put it in the hotel safe."

"But, monsieur, I have my work to do," the maid protested.

"It will only take a minute." He looked inside the handbag, just to be sure she hadn't bought a new one and changed everything. Yes, he recognized those brown envelopes with the traveler's checks, and her passport case and wallet. Was it Henri who had taken her away? Or was she already dead?

The maid, clearly frightened at what they were doing, accompanied him down to the desk, where he explained as much as he could, without giving anything away, to a skeptical concierge, who reluctantly took the handbag from him and, under Marius's watchful eye, stowed it in the safe.

"Now," said Marius, after the maid had been allowed to return to her work, "tell me, did anyone see her go out?" He described Jessica, without knowing what she had been wearing, and received a negative answer. Of course, she was only a grain of sand in this big hotel. And she might have gone out last night before this crew came on duty.

He asked everyone at the desk. All he had to go on was what she had been wearing yesterday, her yellow slacks and a flowered shirt.

Yes, said a clerk, he remembered some yellow slacks. This morning.

Anyone could have yellow slacks, sniffed the concierge. These were all tourists. They favored bright colors.

"Was she young?" Marius asked the clerk, "with reddish hair down to here?" Vaguely he indicated his shoulder.

"The hair, yes," said the clerk, "and I think young, but she wore big, round sunglasses. You couldn't see her face very well. She went out about nine o'clock, with two men."

"And the men?"

"Dark," was all the clerk had noticed. Dark, like almost everyone else in Provence. "One had on a suit," he added. "Like yours."

It would be Henri. He always wore a suit. In gratitude, Marius pressed two ten-franc pieces into the man's hand. Of all the people swarming in and out of the lobby, to have noticed Jessica. But then, she was very pretty. And those bright yellow trousers.

He returned to his car and sat inside it for a moment, trying to think what he should do. Find Henri, of course, but where? The most obvious place was his flat in Vence, but he had not been there recently, simply because it *was* the most obvious place.

And why the hell had he taken Jessica? What did he want with her? He could go to hell and back, or even to Aden, as far as Marius was concerned, if he hadn't taken Jessica. Of course, the police still wanted him for those bombs, and eventually they would find him, but the bombs were *fait accompli*, while Jessica was still very much in danger.

Angrily he started the engine and drove to the police station, only to find that it was their damnable lunch hour. One officer was still there. Marius told him what had happened to Jessica.

"But, monsieur," the officer said reasonably, "have you any proof that the lady was taken against her will?"

He had known that was coming. Of course he had no proof. His knowledge, his suspicions, did not count.

"She left her handbag," he said. "I found it in her room. It's now in the hotel safe. No woman goes off without her handbag."

Probably true, but still not proof. He told the policeman about the bombings. There was no evidence tying them to Henri, except that one of them had happened in Henri's laboratory. He mentioned the time Henri had abducted Jessica in his car. He had threatened her then, but had not harmed her.

The policeman wrote it all down. He nodded obligingly, his mind on lunch.

"The man has been seen around Nice," Marius offered. "He has a flat in Vence, but he hasn't been there in at least a week. Of course the police in Grasse are looking for him, too, because of that bombing."

"He will be found," the officer said, nodding again, this time with certainty.

"And the girl, in the meantime?"

"One thing I don't understand," said the policeman, tapping his lower lip with his pen, "why would Monsieur Harger take the girl in the first place? And from her hotel room?"

"I have no idea." Marius was getting tired of this. Why was it his job to explain motivations? "They want something they think she has. A picture with an important message on it. They searched her room in another hotel." Again no proof that it was they who had done it.

"Excuse me," he said finally, "I've wasted enough time. While I stay here talking to you, no one is looking for her. She could be in very great danger."

The policeman made no effort to persuade him to stay. He was just a nuisance with this alarmist story.

Again Marius got into his car. The next stop, he decided, would be Vence. He was not sure exactly why, but he had to start somewhere.

He sped up the road into the hills. There was a strong possibility that he might be leaving her back in Nice, but what could he do? Nice was a sizable city. He had no idea where to begin looking.

Sometime later, after parking a block away from Henri's house, he approached the building by walking close to its wall, so as not to be seen by anybody watching from the top floor.

He knocked at the door that he assumed belonged to the concierge. There was no reply. Damn, he thought, and knocked again. Then he began to climb the stairs.

On the last flight, he heard sounds coming from Henri's apartment. The door was open. Great God, had he caught them?

His first glimpse showed him that the flat was empty. A woman whom he took to be the concierge was cleaning a window while a well-formed, empty-eyed, younger version of her swept the floor.

"Where is Monsieur Harger?" Marius demanded from the doorway.

The young woman gave him a slow, charming smile. "He's gone. We're fixing the apartment to rent it again."

Gone? Furniture and all?

"Do you know where he went?"

"No, monsieur, he left no address."

"None at all? What about his mail?"

The girl shrugged. It was not her problem what happened to Monsieur Harger's mail.

"What did he do with his furniture?" Not that it was important, but he needed time to adjust to this.

"A truck came and took it away." This information was followed by another sleepy smile.

Alerted, he asked, "Did the truck have anything written on it? Where it was from?"

The girl shook her head. "It was only a big gray truck." She stopped and played with the broom for a moment. A vacuum cleaner stood in the corner, but they had to sweep up the debris first.

"It looked," she continued idly, "just like the truck I saw outside his farmhouse once."

"What farmhouse?"

The girl's mother evidently wondered, too. She glanced sharply at her daughter.

The girl seemed to realize, in her slow way, that she had

163

been indiscreet. She moved closer to Marius.

"You know," she said quietly, "that place he has out in the country. I don't think he ever stays there, but he keeps it. It's a nice place to go."

"I don't know it," Marius said. "I've never been there. Can you tell me where it is?"

"Oh, not really. It's out in the mountains. There's a very steep hill that goes down."

He nodded intently. The entire area, for hundreds of kilometers, consisted of very steep hills.

"Which direction do you go?"

"Oh, monsieur." The question was evidently beyond her, but she did her best. "You know this street out here? You go to the end of it and then you turn this way." Her right. He was about to ask which end of the street. It made a big difference. Then she added, "You go toward Tourette. Past it, I think."

"Is it this side of the Loup?"

"I don't remember. I'm sorry, monsieur."

My God, he thought, she doesn't even remember crossing the river. What a man Henri must be.

"And then?"

"That's all I know. It's near a very steep hill." The girl's voice dropped with finality.

"You say it's out in the country. There's no village nearby? Nothing?"

"Oh, yes, some olive trees. A lot of olive trees. And a broken stone wall. That's where the road goes in. You can't see the house from the road, it's behind some trees."

He was to look for olive trees, which grew in profusion along those roads, and a broken stone wall. That might be easier, if it were very noticeable from the road.

He thanked the girl and, unseen by her mother, slipped her a ten-franc note.

164

18

Jessica woke slowly, fighting the wakefulness. Her pain was too much to bear. She lay twisted on the floor, her arms tied behind her. The right arm, under her body, was numb. Her head pounded and her stomach churned.

Gradually she rolled her weight off the numb arm. Her hands broke free.

She brought them in front of her and stared at the rope trailing from her left wrist. She had cut it, now she remembered. She had sawed the rope on that stone up there. And then had passed out.

She sat up. Her head felt better once she was upright, except for a throbbing on the side that had hit the floor. She listened and heard nothing, only a light breeze in the leaves outside the window. She was soaked with sweat, but oddly, the room was somewhat cool, perhaps because of the stone walls.

Her arm began to thaw. She clutched at it, gritting her teeth and holding her breath against the pain. After a while the terrible ache subsided. Her fingers still felt tender. In a minute she could begin to work on the ropes that bound her feet.

The next step would be to find something with which to gouge through the door. It might take days. She remembered, in *The Count of Monte Cristo,* the Abbé Faria, who had devoted ages to digging at his cell wall, only to break

165

through at last and find that he was in another cell instead of outside.

Here, it was only a wooden door. Not so difficult, as long as you had something to attack it with. Impossible, if you did not.

She began to pick at her ropes. The men must have gone. There was no sound except the rustle of wind. Gone and left her here. She supposed that leaving her here to die was slightly more legal than killing her outright.

She imagined her body lying in that room, decomposing, until someone found her. She saw it all dispassionately. It did not upset or frighten her. Even her parents— they would get over it. They had each other, and the store. After the initial shock, they would probably think it inevitable that something had happened to her in this queer region, with these unpredictable people.

Her brain cleared a little more, and she thought: *They won't know who I am.* She had no identification. Her passport and everything else had been left in her hotel room. Right this minute, somebody was probably stealing her cash and traveler's checks.

Her fingers were nimble now. She struggled with the knots at her ankles and finally untied them.

She wobbled to her feet, stumbled a few times, and at last was standing, holding the wall for support. The plaster felt cool. She rested her forehead against it, then staggered to the bed and lay down.

When her nausea and dizziness receded, she sat up and looked out of the window above the bed. Just outside was a tree with gently waving leaves. Beyond it the earth sloped sharply and finally disappeared, perhaps into that deep gorge she had noticed on the way here. She could not see any other houses, or any sign of human life.

But she knew there was human life around here, so if she could only get out of the house . . .

She stood up again slowly, giving herself time to gather

strength in her legs, and finally walked across the room to the door. She listened, and again heard nothing.

The door did not have a knob, only a pull handle. A very odd door. How did they latch it? She tugged at the handle, but the door did not move.

She looked into the keyhole and saw blackness. That probably meant the key was there. She was surprised at their carelessness. Didn't they know that very elementary trick?

She searched the room for a piece of paper, and couldn't find one. She would have to use the cloth with which they had gagged her. It was soft and might only bunch together on the rough floor. She unfolded it and gently slipped it under the door. Fortunately the gap between door and floor was a wide one. She only hoped the men were far away, and could not see or hear her.

Then, for a moment, she was stumped. She needed something with which to push out the key. A pencil, a bobby pin, anything. There was nothing. She took one of the ropes that had bound her, twisted its end in her mouth until it was damp and as stiff as she could make it. She poked it into the keyhole.

It stuck. She had to peel off some of the strands and repeat the twisting process. Then she tried again.

The rope was soft and weak. She pushed more and more of it into the hole. Finally she heard the key fall down onto the cloth and carefully pulled it toward her under the door.

She unlocked the door, opened it a few inches, and listened. Again she heard the rustle of leaves and grass, and felt moving air. There were windows open. She pulled the door farther open and stepped outside.

She was in a small entryway. Across from her, evidently, was the living room. It held a fireplace, two comfortable chairs, and, in one corner, a large table. To her right was the front door. It was heavy wood with a small, round window.

There was no one in the living room. She saw no one when she peered through the round window in the front door.

They would not have gone off and left all the windows open. Maybe they meant to come back.

Cautiously she clicked the latch on the door, and slowly opened it. The afternoon heat struck her face. The leaves and grasses were quiet now. There was nothing but heat. She stepped down onto the flat stone below the doorsill and started toward the corner of the house.

A sudden, blinding terror. She screamed.

It was Fayez. He carried a rifle, and looked almost as startled as she.

Jessica turned quickly, stupidly. She ought to have run toward him. Then he would have had to turn before he could fire. It was too late now. She saw the ground drop sharply below her. A steep, steep hill. Hard to run. And few trees. No shelter.

Marius, she thought as she stumbled.

Marius had almost reached Grasse. Damn that girl.

He couldn't damn her. She had done her best. How could she have known that someone's life might someday depend upon her knowing where the farmhouse was? She knew Henri, but could not imagine the world he lived in. No one had done that.

What now? Back across the river and up the other side? It still seemed likely that it was somewhere between Grasse and Vence. Henri must have had a place closer to the factory than his apartment, rather than make that long, winding drive every day. The gasoline alone would—

It reminded him to check the gas gauge. Lucky thing he did. It was getting low for driving around on these empty roads. Perhaps it hadn't been full when he took the car. It should have been. Or maybe he had been driving more than he thought.

He would have to find a station. That was a stupid loss of time, but it would be worse to run out of gas in the middle of nowhere.

Besides, what proof did he have that she was at the farmhouse anyway? It was only a guess.

19

Again she stumbled, twisting her ankle. She caught herself and ran on. He shouted after her. She did not understand.

Then, *"Arrêtez! Arrêtez!"*

Never, never would she stop.

Suddenly the entire gorge echoed with a crash. A puff of earth burst in front of her. The sound almost startled her into falling. Still she ran, hampered by the steep incline, her back prickling in anticipation of the next shot.

Instead, something barreled into her legs and threw her to the ground. She gasped, the air knocked out of her. He slapped her shoulders, helping her to catch a breath.

"I don't want to hurt you," he said in clumsy French, "but you have to stay up there." He pointed to the farm-house.

He helped her up. She tried to brush the powdered earth from her yellow slacks. With his arm supporting her, they started up the hill.

You don't want to hurt me. Then what do you want?

"Que désirez?" she managed to ask.

He tried to speak. His French failed him. He put a finger to her lips.

To keep her from talking. Was that all?

They reached the top of the hill just as a small gray truck rounded the bend. For a moment, she felt hope. But it was their truck. It drew up to a cellar door, and Weyland

and the man with the sunglasses climbed out. Weyland, for once, was not wearing his dapper suit. He had changed to something that looked like army fatigues.

"So," he said, "you tried to get away."

She did not answer. Her only feeling was a dull ache, not even acute enough to be called despair.

"We will soon be on our way," he told her. "You will then have some change of the scenery. In the meantime, please do not make trouble."

She asked, "Are you ever going to let me go?"

"That," he said, as he started toward the cellar, "is something I do not discuss with you."

She ran after him. "Weyland, listen. Listen to me. I can tell you something you want to know."

He paused and looked at her without expression. "Now? You have something to tell me now? I asked you last night for your information. You had much time then to tell me everything but, at the moment, it seems I am busy." He turned away.

"I didn't think—" Desperately she followed him, pleading. "I didn't think it was important. I thought it never worked out. But I know who her contact was. At least the first one."

"First one?" His eyes narrowed.

"Yes, because— well, Marius told me. He said she wanted to export some things, and he introduced her to someone who could help her with shipping. But later that person told him it came to nothing. So I thought— I didn't think that was the person you were looking for, but maybe it is."

She had his attention now. "And who is this person you speak of?"

"It's someone I think you know. And I—I'll make a bargain with you."

"No bargains." With a contemptuous exclamation and wave of his hand, he turned his attention to the cellar, where Fayez and the third man were bringing up more kegs and loading them into the truck. Weyland called something to the men, probably exhorting them to hurry.

She had lost her final chance. Even last night, it might have worked. She had not been sure of it then, had not finished thinking through about Claude Augustín's connection. She had had other things on her mind. Now, if he was still interested, it was probably mostly a matter of academic curiosity.

She watched them. All three were occupied. She could have slipped away. She imagined herself slipping away, but they would notice immediately. They would catch her or shoot her. Where would she go in this wilderness of mountains?

She took a step backward, and again saw herself running down the road. And then what? They knew this area better than she did.

Suddenly Fayez was beside her. Grasping her arm, he lifted her into the back of the truck. He directed her to sit on a matted, soiled cushion, while he himself curled up on what appeared to be a folded coat. The two rear doors were slammed shut and latched. She found herself in stifling near-darkness, the only light coming from a small window at the back of the cab.

"My God," she exclaimed, indicating the kegs of powder. "*C'est le plastique—et nous.*"

"*Ce n'est pas plastique,*" Fayez answered with a smile.

She did not care about the literal composition of it. *Plastique* had been the only word she knew. What were they doing, locked in tight with at least twenty small kegs of explosives?

She remembered that Weyland had claimed it was particularly stable in shipment. She thought again of her parents. Whatever happened, as long as she was not blown to bits, at least she still had a chance.

After an interval, during which they were probably

closing the windows and making fast the cottage, the other two men got into the cab. Weyland, in the driver's seat, started the engine. As they backed around on the rough terrain, the kegs, which she now saw were lashed to the walls of the truck, wobbled dangerously. She tried to remember whether the road was smooth.

But which road? She had no idea where they were going, or even where they were now.

Marius turned his car back toward Vence. It was idiotic, searching these mountains for a house you couldn't even see from the road. Perhaps he should have gone north from Vence in the first place, instead of west.

And maybe he was wasting this whole day in a useless search. They could be anywhere. Anywhere in southern France, or—anywhere.

Before he reached the Loup, he saw another, smaller road branching off to the left. He hadn't tried that one before. Hadn't even noticed it. He had been too preoccupied with watching for the stupid girl's broken stone wall.

Olive trees. They were everywhere. He remembered thinking that when she mentioned it. Not great groves of them, just a few here and there. Would he even see the stone wall? He would have to drive slowly, and there was a car close in back of him. He pulled to the side of the road and waved it to pass, carefully watching the driver's face as it did so. It was not Henri.

Now he could continue at his own speed. Which side? She had not said, and he had been in too much of a hurry to think of asking. It was lucky, anyway, that Henri took a little time out for pleasure. Otherwise Marius would never have known of the place.

He almost slammed on the brake. At first it hadn't looked like a wall, just a tumbled pile of stones. But there it was, with a badly rutted dirt road cutting through

173

it. He felt a surge of elation as he turned quickly onto the new road, driving cautiously now. As soon as he caught a glimpse of the house he would park the car and proceed on foot.

It took him by surprise, for it blended into its setting and was still partially hidden by trees. He stopped and got out of the car. What if they came up behind him and found his car blocking the road?

He hadn't time to worry about that. At least Henri would not recognize this rented car. He wore his dark jacket, even though it was hot, for dark was a better camouflage; and he began walking carefully, keeping to the bushes at the side of the road, watching for motion or any sign of life.

Watching at least for a car. A big gray truck.

He was almost in full sight of the house. There was nothing. No vehicle. And yet it was isolated. If they were here at all, they would need a vehicle.

Maybe in back? But there were trees and bushes in the way. Nothing could have driven there. And the windows of the house were closed.

Of course. It was a stone house. It would be cooler that way.

He studied the ground, the weeds that were packed and matted in the dirt road, unrisen yet, as though wheels had passed over them only a short time ago.

He began to walk quickly, holding up his arms in a sign of surrender. It might gain him a little time, for Henri, after all, was his friend. He wouldn't— But there had been Françoise.

"Henri!" he called. "Henri, are you there?"

His only answer was a flutter of silver leaves.

He reached the front door. "Henri!"

He tried the latch. It was locked.

He peered in one of the windows. A pleasant little house, if sparsely furnished. But no one was there.

174

Quickly he examined the outside for any possible clues.

Something heavy had been here, with wide tires, according to the flattened appearance of the weeds and grasses. The big gray truck? How could they get a big truck along these mountain roads? Maybe it was not so big, and the girl had only exaggerated, or thought any truck was big. It was certain that Henri hadn't taken the furniture, or planned to, for nothing was packed or organized. He hadn't even used the truck to bring his furniture from Vence. None of it was here. What, then?

The cellar door. It had a heavy lock. Not a padlock, but one that had been specially installed. No one would need to lock a cellar door unless he stored something valuable inside. It was not, evidently, the type of cellar that gave access to the house.

He tested the lock. It was not fastened now. The door opened into black nothingness. Surprisingly, the cellar had a concrete floor, not an earthen one, as one would expect in such an old house, and something had recently been scraped across it. He could see a faint gleam, as from new metal.

So Henri had stored something here, something metallic, and had loaded it into what appeared to be a truck—from the looks of the grass, only this afternoon. He had been here and left, possibly just before Marius came.

Was Jessica with him? And where had they gone?

He closed the cellar door and hurried back to his car. Where could Henri have gone, he wondered again. Jessica had seen possibilities in the Yemenite connection.

(Might Jessica have been swept into this of her own will, as apparently Françoise had been? Another dangerously romantic young woman? No, he didn't think so. She would not have gone off without her pocketbook.)

In any case, Henri was taking his cargo somewhere. If Jessica was correct, as seemed likely, he would be taking it to the destination that had been intended all along. To Yemen.

175

So, thought Marius as he started the car, we look for a seaport.

That was a brilliant idea, except that the entire Côte d'Azur was lined with seaports.

Some had better harbors than others. Some had bigger harbors, where an individual boat of questionable credentials might not be so conspicuous. Noticed, of course, for all harbors had their regulations, but able to keep a lower profile.

He drove toward the house, turned around in the area where the truck had been loaded, and started off: to find a harbor in all these hundreds of kilometers of seacoast, to find a boat that he would not recognize even when he saw it—to find it before it was too late.

And they were far ahead of him.

20

They kept her hidden in a cramped, stuffy apartment, guarded by a man she had not seen before. Either they needed Fayez for something else or they thought he had become too friendly with her.

They won't kill me, she thought. I'll just die along with the rest of them. I'll die in Yemen.

She could not begin to imagine such a place. She saw endless sands.

"It's not my fight," she told the burly man with the impassive face, who guarded her. The face remained impassive.

"You don't speak English, do you?" she asked him. He was capable of staring at her with large, dark eyes until she turned away. She tried a phrase in French and received the same stare. He would not be drawn into conversation in any language.

He reacted only to the sound of muffled footsteps on the stairs. Quickly crossing to the door, he put his ear against it and listened. He must have known whose sneakered feet those were.

The footsteps stopped outside the door and a voice mumbled through the crack. After a brief exchange, her guard unfastened dual locks to admit the man who wore sunglasses.

He wore them even now. It must still be daylight outside. She could not tell, for the blackout curtains on the window kept out any semblance of light.

The two men conferred, glancing at her from time to time. Then her guard led her into the hallway and she saw that the stairs were dark. It was nighttime, the sunglasses notwithstanding. The other man turned off the single dim bulb in the room, closed the door without locking it—probably because they never expected to come back—and they started down the stairs.

Outside, a car stood waiting. It was not Weyland's car. That would have been traceable.

They hustled her into it and began a winding, twisting drive through dark streets and around corners. From time to time she glimpsed the harbor, but they did not seem to be heading toward it. Were they planning to leave her somewhere? Alive, or dead?

Finally they drew into a blind alley near the waterfront, and she knew they had only been cautious.

Fayez appeared at the window and handed her guard a dark bundle. He passed it to Jessica, indicating with gestures that she was to put it on. She unfurled it. A long black raincoat.

So that no one could see her bright clothes. Would anyone recognize them, or care?

She managed to slide her arms into the sleeves while sitting down. As she got out of the car they surrounded her, adjusting the coat so that she was concealed as much as possible.

She wondered again at her passivity. Yet it would have been useless to resist. There were three of them. The burly guard did not even need his knife. He could break her in half with his hands.

They left the car and walked out toward the wharfs. How could they do this? she wondered. How could they load a ship with explosives, right under the noses of the Coast Guard, or whatever they had in this country? How could they load a contraband person?

But no one stopped them. The men rushed her along so fast that she had to watch her feet to keep from tripping, and scarcely saw where they were taking her. She was aware only of the boats on either side, and the lights. Yes, there were lights. Why couldn't anyone see?

A dark hulk loomed before her. She was half lifted, half pushed on board. A black ship with no lights. It seemed almost a ghost ship, except for the activity. The deck was alive with men, the three who had brought her and several others. She did not see Weyland.

Someone opened a door and they hurried her down a narrow, ladderlike flight of steps. Her long raincoat tangled under her foot. She clung to the railing and a strong hand caught her elbow. She looked back, but did not recognize the face.

They closed her into a tiny room. At first she could see nothing. It didn't matter; her only thought was escape. She tried the door. Of course they had locked it.

A light went on somewhere outside and shone faintly through the porthole. Now she could see that the room was furnished with four bunk beds and a chest. A crew's room. Did they expect her to stay in here with the crew?

Stay! They couldn't really be taking her away. Not really. She only wanted to be back on shore, driving through the mountains in the sunshine with Marius. Lying on the beach with Steve. Home with her parents. No one would ever know what happened to her.

Even now, who would know? The hotel wouldn't care if she never returned to her room. Marius would be busy with Simone. Her parents would simply think she had no time to write, or her postcards had been delayed, and when they finally started to worry, it would be too late.

It was already too late . . . too late . . . too late . . .

Again she tried the door. Locked fast. She tugged at the porthole. It had a latch, but would not open. She could not have crawled through it anyway. It was much too small, like the windows at the farmhouse.

The room was tight and airless. She could hardly breathe. A rivulet of sweat trickled down her spine. She sloughed off the clammy raincoat.

Through the porthole she could see other ships, and lights, but no people. There must be people out there. If only she could signal. That was one thing that could be said for smoking. She would have had a cigarette lighter or a match.

No, she wouldn't, because she didn't have her purse.

She could pretend. Ask Weyland for a cigarette. Then set fire to something. Her bra. Anything. There wasn't even bedding on those bunks.

She couldn't breathe.

Suddenly the ship began to rumble. Her first thought was the explosives. She grabbed for the edge of a bunk. Then she realized it was the engines.

No, she thought. *No.*

She was not sure when they started to move. It began imperceptibly as they eased out of the berth.

She heard voices speaking French. The Coast Guard! Then it occurred to her that they were Weyland's men, simply trying to be unnoticeable.

She pounded on the door. "I can't breathe! Please let me out, I can't breathe!"

She could not remember how to say "breathe" in French. "I need air!" she called to them. "It's too hot in here. I'm dying."

The door opened.

"So you are dying?" Weyland inquired. "At a time like this?" A time of fulfillment for him, but not for her. "Why don't you open the window?"

"I can't. It's stuck."

He looked at the porthole and then at her. He took her wrist and held it tightly while he opened the porthole latch, pulled at it, and pounded futilely, trying to loosen the heavy frame.

"Can't I come up on deck now that we've started?" she asked.

He regarded her for a moment, trying to make up his mind.

"If you will put on your coat," he decided.

She put on the coat but did not fasten it.

"Thank you, Weyland. I know you're really a decent person."

"Yes, you see? I could have had you killed." As though to prove how decent he was. She nodded dumbly and preceded him up the steps, holding the raincoat high so it would not trip her again.

At the top of the steps they were greeted by an excited babble of Arabic. Weyland, temporarily distracted by whatever news was being imparted, did not notice when she slipped past him onto the deck.

She followed the direction they were watching and pointing.

Lights. A boat. A small one, and coming fast.

Weyland called something down the steps. Almost instantly the engines rumbled louder. The deck trembled and the ship picked up speed.

The small boat blinked a light at them.

Then a voice, amplified, but still faint.

"Henri! Henri!"

It couldn't be Marius.

"Henri, do you have the girl? Let her go!"

Marius.

She understood now why she was there. What if someone shot at them? A cargo of explosives . . .

Weyland turned to her. "Go inside!"

She did not move. In an instant she thought of those powerful engines. She saw the wake they churned in back of the ship. How did it work? Would it suck her in?

She had no more time to think. She was out of the rain-coat.

Over the rail, balanced for a moment—A few deep breaths, and she leaped.

The water boiled around her, black and light. Through it, she heard the thundering of the engines.

Still submerged, she pushed herself in the direction of her dive. At any moment she expected to be pulled backward, slashed and mangled.

Her breath gave out. She fought against taking another. Whatever was up there, she must let herself float to the surface.

An eternity of dying. Finally her head broke through the water. She felt air on her face. Saw the stars. The sky. She swallowed gulps of air.

Lights were bearing down on her. She turned her head. Couldn't see the black ship.

Marius. Marius was here. The lights were almost above her.

She began to struggle in the water. Pushed herself backward. The boat receded.

People watched her from the low deck. She could not see Marius. A man called to her and threw a life preserver.

Her hand splashed into the water. It missed the floating ring. She looked up at the stars and struggled, her legs pumping. She was moving away from the life preserver.

She could hear the boat's engine, barely chugging as it hovered near her, trying to reach her.

They couldn't see her legs. She kicked as though paddling in place. From the position of the boat, she knew she was moving back toward shore.

They pulled in the life preserver and threw it again. Slowly they turned the boat. Now she could see him.

"Zhessica!" he called. One of the men seemed to be holding him back.

The preserver had almost struck her. She reached out

her hand and touched it. Then her hand slipped off it and she floated away.

"Marius!" she called. Her mouth filled with water. She spat it out. "Don't worry. I'm coming."

She reached again for the life preserver. Again she floated away. Was she still moving toward the shore?

They called instructions to her. One of the men took off his shoes. Getting ready to come in after her.

She lifted a tired arm just as they pulled in the life preserver for the second time. She beckoned for them to throw it again and hoped they would understand.

This time she caught it. They motioned for her to slip it over her head. She put her arm through it instead and signaled that she was ready.

She felt a tightening of the line. Within moments, they had drawn her to the side of the boat. Hands reached out for her. She let go of the preserver and bobbed away from them. She splashed and struggled, grabbed for the helping hands, missed, choked on salt water, and grabbed again.

They shouted encouragement. She could not catch the words, they were all talking at once in French, but she knew by the tone that they were trying to give advice. She nodded, she did understand that much, and reached for them again. A hand grasped her wrist so that her enfeebled arm could not slip away, and they pulled her into the boat.

Marius was there beside her. She saw concern in his dark eyes. They were all speaking to her, but she was too busy choking to be able to listen.

Marius patted her on the back. "They want to know," he translated, "which way was the ship going?"

She raised her head, looked around, and in the distance, saw the harbor lights. That would be north.

"Quick, Zhessica." He didn't care that she had nearly drowned, that water was still in her mouth and throat, that she had been kidnapped and almost dragged to the end of the earth.

She stood with her back to the harbor and considered, then raised a shaky hand.

"To the *west*?" he asked incredulously. "How can that be?"

She choked again and cleared her throat. Her voice came out almost a whisper.

"They swung to the right when they got out of the harbor. I heard them talking about Morocco."

"They spoke French?"

"Of course. What else? Marius, I'm freezing."

Her last sentence was lost as orders were shouted back and forth and the engines picked up power. She had wanted to go inside the cabin to warm up, but could not, now. She had to see what they were doing.

"Morocco?" Marius asked above the engine noise. "You are sure of that?"

"Oh, yes!"

"But, Henri—" He stared at her, puzzled. Henri had no ties to Morocco.

"I'm only telling you what happened," she said, and watched the boat plunge ahead into empty darkness.

After bagging nothing more than a large white yacht heading for Monte Carlo, they turned back to the harbor. She allowed herself one brief look to the east. Somewhere out there was a black ship with fast engines and no lights, on its way toward the Suez Canal.

Well, she thought, as someone belatedly produced a blanket to wrap her in, I did what I could.

When the boat landed, there were questions, an official report to be filled out, but they made it as brief as possible. She finally relinquished the blanket and Marius turned on the heater in his car as he drove her to the Hôtel Côte d'Azur.

"Are you sure you want to stay there?" he asked. "You won't be afraid?"

"Why should I be afraid? They've gone, haven't they?

Marius, how did you ever find me? How did you know they had me?"

He smiled slightly, but there was little humor in it.

"It was not easy. I have been looking for you the whole day. As for knowing they had you, we can thank the sharp eyes and fine memory of a clerk at your hotel, who deserves more than the twenty francs I gave him. And that reminds me, your handbag is in the strongbox of the hotel. That is how I knew you were captured."

His manner was cool. She had kept him from Simone. But it wasn't her fault. He must understand that it wasn't her fault.

He procured the handbag for her and insisted upon taking her upstairs to her room. He also insisted upon searching it carefully.

"It's really all right, Marius," she said. "They *have* gone. We saw them go, didn't we? And don't worry, I'll keep the balcony door shut tonight. I'm so cold I don't want any fresh air."

"Yes, you are cold," he agreed. "You must take a warm bath at once and go to bed."

She was further chilled by his attitude, but only as he was about to leave did she understand the reason for it.

"Tell me one thing, Zhessica," he said, his hand on the doorknob. "Why did you let them get away?"

"Let them—get away?"

"Yes. You will pardon me, but you were clumsy when the Coast Guard tried to pull you from the water. Very clumsy. You could not catch the—what do you call that thing?"

"Life preserver."

"You were almost fighting it. I noticed. I hope they did not. And then that silly story about Morocco. Zhessica!"

"But I did think—"

He eyed her suspiciously. "They were really speaking French?"

185

"No. Arabic. I didn't understand one word. But, Marius, after all that, I couldn't let them be stopped."

"After all what?"

"They worked so hard, they had such hope, and going off in a little black boat to fight for their country—You know what they're up against. I mean, it's so brave."

"Well," he said, apparently startled by her passion, "what about the people at the factory? And Françoise, and Simone?"

Françoise . . . Could she tell him? Not now. Certainly not now. But the rest—

"It wasn't Henri," she answered quietly. "They took his shipments. It was someone—someone who they thought was helping. That was Françoise's exporting business. They sent his explosives to their own people. Everything that happened, they made it look as if the rebels did it. Henri found out. Françoise was supposed to get evidence about who these people were, and I was supposed to be carrying that evidence."

"The picture?" he asked.

"Yes, but—"

"The picture was only Françoise."

"You said there might have been something in the message." She wished she could have told him all this without discussing the picture. It would only be worse for him, knowing the truth.

"I can think of nothing," he said, "except the Spanish. There is someone with a Spanish name . . ."

"Who is that?"

"Claude Augustín."

"That's Spanish?"

"The way he spells it, it is Spanish. In French it is pronounced the same, but we spell it t-i-n-e. I have been finding out about him. I have asked the questions, and I learned that he was born in Spain, but his family left many years ago, at the time of their civil war. Probably they were Communists. All right, I don't mind if his family were Communists, but what he does, to think that he is involved with this, it is hard for me to believe. He is a good friend, especially of my mother."

"And he's the one—"

The look on his face stopped her from saying more.

"I don't want to think about that. Not at this time."

He spoke almost angrily. She knew how he must feel. If tragedy had come about because of the meeting he had arranged between his sister and Augustín, he would have to face it gradually, in his own way.

"Zhessica, your teeth are beginning to shake. You had better take off these wet clothes."

"You're right. I'd better."

She could hear her clock ticking, but could not see it. She felt disoriented. This day had been two days long.

Her teeth still chattered, but he quieted them for a moment by taking her head in his hands and placing a kiss on her mouth. It began as a quick kiss, but it lingered. She could feel herself melting, and then he put her away from him.

"Get some sleep, Zhessica. I have more work to do. Good night."

21

She woke in the morning, startled and terrified, as some-one knocked on her door.

"*Qui est-ce?*" she asked, and received an outpouring in Italian. During its course she remembered that Weyland was somewhere southeast on the Mediterranean and would not bother her again.

She asked in French for a clarification of what had been said. This time she learned that the maid wanted to know whether she was ready to have her room cleaned.

"*Absolutement non,*" she replied. "I just woke up. Thank you anyway."

She looked at the clock. It was almost noon. No won-der the maid had been concerned. She turned over, facing the murky light that shone through the green plastic blinds, and tried to sleep again.

Her mind grew crowded with memories and impressions. This whole trip . . . her innocent vacation.

But she was safe now. If it hadn't been for Marius, the Coast Guard never would have found her. They would not even have known enough to look for her. She could hard-ly have swum that distance back to the harbor.

She sat up and counted the days. This was Saturday, her last full day in Nice. Tomorrow she would leave for Marseilles. The rest of her trip would be an anticlimax after Nice, but one she would welcome wholeheartedly.

She would miss Marius, and tried to tell herself it was only because he had been a good friend. When she thought of him, she would see him by Simone's bedside at the hospital, but Simone would appear as she had on that day in the mountains, wearing her white dress and pink coat—the day before the first bomb.

The telephone rang.

Marius, she thought, and eagerly picked it up.

"Hi, there, stranger," said a decidedly un-French voice. "I'll bet you don't remember me."

"Steve! My heavens! Where are you?"

"Right here in town. Just passing through. And where are you? You're not at the Foster any more, what happened?"

"How did you ever find me?" The same question she had asked Marius.

"Just figured I'd start calling every hotel in town. Lucky you picked one near the beginning of the alphabet. You didn't even leave a forwarding address."

"But how did you know I was still in Nice?"

"Took a chance. You said you were going to be here a week. How about getting together?"

"Well, I—"

"Don't tell me you have to wash your hair."

She touched her hair, which she had not washed last night, in her hurry to get to bed. It was sticky with salt.

"I could do that right now," she said, thinking it would be fun to see Steve. She had hoped to hear from Marius, but last night he had acted as though he had seen more than enough of her.

She agreed, regretting her hesitation. There was no reason to hurt Steve's feelings.

"But let's make it kind of early," she suggested. "I really have to pack and get ready."

"Okay. There's this place called the Cave. It's near the harbor." He gave her the address. "Meet me there at eight."

Eight o'clock. She could pack most of her things in the afternoon, and have a leisurely day, with no pressures.

She got up and opened the blinds. There was the little park, and the palm trees. The bright sunshine. The Mediterranean, peaceful and blue, and dotted with sailboats and pedal boats.

She had stripped and was ready to turn on the shower when the telephone rang again. Wrapping herself in a towel, although no one could see into her room, she ran to answer it.

"What are you doing?" Marius asked.

She pulled the towel tighter.

"I was about to wash my hair. It's still got salt in it."

"So I didn't wake you. And you are feeling all right?"

"Yes, of course."

"I forgot. You were not as tired as you pretended to be."

And that, she could tell by his tone, still rankled. He went on, "You are planning to go away tomorrow? I would like to see you before you leave. Could we have dinner tonight?"

Damn, she thought, why couldn't he have called first?

"I'm sorry. I already . . . that American I met on the train. He's taking me out. I don't even know where to reach him."

"It's all right," Marius said calmly. "If not tonight, then tomorrow I will drive you to Marseilles. Yes? You are not already engaged to drive to Marseilles?"

"Oh, no, that would be wonderful. I'd love it."

She would see him again. A ride all the way to Marseilles. And no fears hanging over them.

Only, she remembered, Simone. But that would not spoil the ride.

As she stepped into the shower, she wondered vaguely why he wanted to take so much trouble. For him, it would be a round trip. Hadn't he already done enough for her?

190

She had not much packing to do, with only her suitcase and flight bag. It had mostly been an excuse for an early evening, for she had known she would probably be tired.

When her hair was dry, she went down to the hotel coffee shop and ordered lunch. It took an hour. There was the rest of the afternoon to get through. An afternoon, evening, and night before that long drive to Marseilles.

And that would be the last she would see of him. She had better start gaining some perspective.

She returned to her room and sat on the balcony, studying her guidebooks, which by now she had nearly memorized. The balcony was a perfect place to while away the afternoon. She could look out at the sea and be thankful that she was saved from it.

She thought of Weyland, and his hopes, and Françoise. She had thought she knew Françoise. Weyland had felt the same way. What made her betray him? Was it force? Blackmail? If she was not already one of them, what had made her kill Bernard Martin, so that then she could be blackmailed?

Or was it conviction? She had certainly spoken sometimes as though she believed in the principles of Marx and Lenin. Jessica remembered how she had talked about the perfume factory and the underpaid young people, and the general inequities of life.

But to betray Weyland? Her friend and possibly her lover? Or maybe she had only been using him all along, seizing on his eagerness to help his country, and turning it against him.

El jefe et moi . . . It was possible that El Jefe was more important than anyone else. She had never identified him, as Weyland had expected, but only pretended to, undoubtedly to save her own skin if the message should fall into Weyland's hands, as well it might have.

Jessica saw Françoise recede farther and farther, the

191

Françoise she had known. And Weyland's Françoise, too, although he had known things about her that Jessica had not. Yet it was because of Françoise that she was here, and that all these things had happened to her. Because of a Françoise that perhaps never existed.

The afternoon sun grew hot. She retired inside, turned on the air conditioner and slept for a while, then went back to the balcony.

She watched a sailboat on the water, a man walking his dog in the park.

Nice . . . She thought she might even miss it.

After a while she changed from her jeans to a flowered print dress and carefully applied her eye makeup. It was five o'clock. She still had three hours.

Even though she had been in Nice for a week, there was so much she hadn't done. There were the places she kept thinking about, the Old Town, and the Château, that nearly vertical mountain that guarded the harbor. In passing it, she had seen people scrambling down endless long steps. It was apparently quite a tourist attraction, and it would be right on her way.

Packing her camera into her purse, she started out to walk through the Old Town.

She was nearly there when she passed what she assumed to be the flower market, rows of long tables under an open-walled roof. It was closed now for the day. She had never gotten to see that well-known feature of Nice, but she had seen the flower farms in the mountains, and maybe that was enough.

She knew the Old Town as soon as she reached it. It had a built-up, closed-in feeling, with streets barely wide enough for one Renault. Even the sidewalks were narrow. If two people happened to be standing and talking, she had to go out into the street to get around them.

Above the shops were tiny dark tenements. The darkness might have been depressing, but it was also, she supposed, cooler. The people who lived there kept their flowers on the windowsills and themselves behind closed blinds.

Before long, she had passed through the Old Town and come out onto the boulevard that swept around the Château to the harbor, and on along the coast.

She looked up at the steps that led from the Château Park, and at the people walking down them. Few were climbing. There must be another way up.

Drawing closer, she noticed a passageway built into the mountain itself. Above the entrance was a sign that said *Ascenseur.* An elevator. She would ride up and walk down.

At the ticket booth she bought a fare for *Montée,* and shook her head when asked if she wanted another for *Descendre.* There were no round-trip tickets, evidently.

She followed a white-tiled, L-shaped tunnel to the elevator. When she rounded the corner, no one else was in sight. Conditioned by the week she had just lived through, she almost backed out, but the only thing that waited for her was the elevator and its operator, a large man in gray shirt and pants, who nodded and mumbled, *"Bonjour."*

The ride was brief. She came out onto a narrow parapet that surrounded the top of the elevator housing. There was no place to go but around to the back of it, where she crossed a tiny bridge and entered the park.

A sign above the path read *Le Parc de Château ferme les portes à 20 heures.* Twenty hours she translated as eight P.M. It was six o'clock now. That left her plenty of time. By eight, she was supposed to meet Steve at the Cave.

She climbed a short flight of steps and found a road that came up from the city. Here was an amusement area with bump cars and a refreshment stand. Beyond it, a children's playground, all paved in sand. It was nearly deserted now.

She walked on to the sea side of the mountain. From

193

there she could look down on all of Nice, which was bisected by the Château. She studied the harbor, trying to figure out where she had been last night, the small, drab room where they had kept her while they loaded the ship. If she had binoculars, she might even be able to see the car they had taken her in, probably still parked in its alleyway, waiting for the police to find it and return it to the rental company.

And what about the farmhouse? she wondered. Who would be using it now? Did Weyland expect to return someday?

She took the camera from her purse and snapped a shot of the harbor. Not that she would ever forget that night. But this, she thought, might give her pleasanter memories.

Tall spikes of agave grew along the edge of the cliff, outside a rail that protected the path. It made a striking foreground for her pictures of the sea and the harbor.

She stopped to change her film, then continued along the path until she overlooked the other side of Nice, the part where her hotel was. She could see the sweep of the shoreline as it curved around the Baie des Anges. She saw the beaches, the blue-green water, the gleaming white-and-pastel city washed by late sunshine.

"*Au revoir*, Nice," she whispered. It was her wish, too, to come back.

She need not, however, have whispered. There was no one to hear her. A few people strolled along the paths in the distance, but soon disappeared, and she was alone again. It surprised her, at this hour of the day. She would have thought everyone would come here to walk before dinner. It was the best part of Nice.

Her watch, which still ran, although erratically, after its immersion in the ocean, said a quarter to seven. She had better start finding her way down.

Since she had not come up by the long flight of steps, she was not sure where they began, but "down" was ob-

194

viously in the direction of the slope toward the main part of Nice.

She started along a descending path, walking down a few broad steps. Then the path forked. One branch seemed to lead downward more steeply than the other. She followed the steeper one and found herself in a cul-de-sac, a pocket that led nowhere, with only a park bench and a few dead leaves on the ground.

She tried the other fork. There, a short flight of steps led back up into the park.

Somewhere along the way she had missed the turn altogether. She retraced her direction and found another path that inclined downward. Confidently she started along it, only to discover that it took her to the elevator and not the steps. And she hadn't a *descendre* ticket.

Perhaps they would let her on if she paid in cash. But there was still time to look for the steps.

If worst came to worst, she thought, there was always the roadway, but she had no idea where it went. It might carry her miles away.

She turned back and again tried the most promising path, which was the way she had gone before. Again there was the dead end, and again the steps leading back up into the park.

The whole thing was getting very silly, frustrating, and a little nerve-wracking. She would have been embarrassed if she thought there was anyone watching her, but no one seemed to be about.

Resolutely she started back to the elevator. If they would not take cash, they could at least tell her where the steps were.

But there was one more chance: a path that seemed to lead away from where she thought the steps might be, but still headed downward. Probably it looped back. She followed it down a few broad steps, past a thick clump of spiky purple flowers, only to find herself in another cul-de-sac.

Here, too, was a pleasant bench, and a railing with a view. She could look over the rail and see Nice. She could see the roofs and balconies of nearby houses, and she knew there were steps that led down into the city. They were somewhere nearby, but invisible.

The evening began to take on a nightmarish quality. There *was* a way out. She knew that. Other people found it. She had seen great streams of people climbing down.

A shoe scraped on the path somewhere in back of her. She turned gratefully from the railing.

"Steve! Of all people! What are you doing here?"

She felt almost dizzy, watching him saunter toward her down the steps, when she had thought she was alone, and was expecting to meet him an hour later at least a kilometer away.

"Sit down," he invited her, gesturing toward the bench.

He took the seat beside her, gave her hand a little squeeze, and smiled.

Jessica said, "I guess it's not too surprising that we ran into each other, considering we were both headed in the same direction, more or less *from* the same direction, I should imagine, even if this is a slight detour. But how did you happen to see me? I didn't see you."

"I doubt if you were looking for me," he replied. "You were too busy trying to find the way out."

Again her redheaded complexion gave her away. She tried to cover her embarrassment by answering airily, "Oh, I was just exploring a little. I was never up here before, and this was my last chance to take some pictures. It's a gorgeous view, isn't it?"

He blinked solemnly at her from behind his glasses. "I'm glad you had such a brilliant idea. It worked out perfectly. Here you are and here I am. And I didn't mean to come to a confrontation, but you're a very slippery young woman, so I'll have to ask you outright. The picture, please."

196

"The—picture?"

She felt the warm air on her face, the edge of the bench against the back of her knees. She raised her head and saw nothing but the mound of purple flowers cutting off her view of the path and everything above it. They were in a nice, secluded spot.

His voice was low and conversational. "You're an intelligent girl. You can figure it out. If you can't, then just hand over your purse. I'll find it."

She looked around at the part of the path that she could see. There was no one. *No one.* They had all gone home to eat. Those gastronomical French. Maybe if she screamed . . .

She watched his hand slowly rise. He held a small vial, like a pocket perfume atomizer.

"It won't do you any good, dear. One whiff of this and you're dead."

Her lips felt dry, numb, unmanageable. "What do you want out of my purse?" She fumbled at the zipper.

"Not your money. It's hardly worth all the trouble I've gone to. Just the picture."

The voice was still smooth, but beneath it she could hear an edge of impatience.

Her only way out was the path. Desperately she glanced at the rail that bordered their pleasant nook. Beyond it the earth dropped away sharply and rockily into the city of Nice.

"Yes," Steve agreed, "it's a long way down. But who here knows anything about you? A hopeless love affair . . . Even a mugger. You remember Françoise, don't you? It could happen anywhere."

He moved the vial back and forth in front of her face. "This is quicker, though. You wouldn't even have time to be afraid, and I think that's better. I really liked you, Jessica. We had a lot of fun together. For a while I thought we might even be able to work together."

The name he had mentioned made a dim connection in her mind. "Like you and—Françoise?"

"Never mind about Françoise."

"She helped you. She sent what you wanted. Why is she dead?"

"I said never mind. It was just a precaution. You can't rely on a person like that. Now hand it over."

Just a precaution. It was a life!

She stared at the vial, remembering that day at the beach.

And other impressions: Simone in the back of the car with her dog. That unbelievable moment at the factory.

Her parents. She could no longer see the airport. Only the two of them, side by side, smiling their love as they launched their only child into the world.

"You can't—" Her voice broke. She remembered the train trip, with all the excitement of travel ahead of her. Steve taking her to lunch, the sun coming out, the umbrella pines. All gone—

"The picture, Jessica."

—because she knew that, even if she could produce the picture, it would be the rail or the vial. If the picture was so important, then so was silence, and not having anyone alive who would know.

Françoise . . .

"Stop wasting time, Jessica. Just give it to me."

"I don't have it with me."

The shadows, the searching. How did he know so much about the picture if he had never seen it?

"What do you mean you don't have it? Where is it?"

"In my room."

She stood up as though to go and get it for him, but she knew that would never be. She would never leave here.

He stood, too. He had no intention of letting her leave.

Through the bushes she glimpsed a flash of color.

If she screamed, even if he killed her, he would be caught.

But would they come? Or run away?

It was a plump, middle-aged woman in a red-and-white dress, walking purposefully down the path.

Not strolling, but purposefully.

Jessica took a step backward, toward the path. Steve followed her, holding up the vial.

She forced herself to look into his eyes. And not breathe. Not breathe.

She let him get close to her. Very close.

Her knee shot up. As he doubled over, she turned and ran.

She had only an instant.

The woman was almost out of sight. But there she was, far ahead, walking up the steps that seemed to lead back into the park.

Jessica was all motion, running and screaming, screaming and running, an image of fire at her back.

She passed the woman, saw alarm on the stolid face. This was their only contact, but to the woman she owed her life. For after the few ascending steps, the path curled around and started down the side of the cliff.

She ran down the steps, all of them, her flimsy sandals threatening to catch or break. She passed startled faces, pushed aside bodies. Where had they all been?

Down the steps. Forever and ever. A gray blur of steps.

Then through the cramped Old Town, dodging cars on narrow streets.

The vial. With the vial he could kill her. A poison gas or spray. No one would know he did it. She dared not take a moment to look back.

Oh please, God, a gendarme. *Please.*

But there were none.

She rounded a corner, saw a café with its door standing open. She slipped inside.

It was dim and smoky, filled with men in work clothes. She could hide here.

But he spoke French better than she did. He would have some story to get her out.

The men watched her, smiling in delighted mystification at her presence.

"Police?" she begged. *"Les gendarmes, s'il vous plait?"*

A chuckle. A shrug. A gesture of empty hands. There were no police in here.

The cashier, long and thin with a fish face, delivered a tumble of directions.

Only six feet away, the door stood open. He would find her. He would be stalking her, waiting just outside.

And the police would never understand her. He would catch her first.

Only one person would understand.

"Telephone?" she asked. "Telephone?"

There had to be one. At home, they would have had a pay phone.

The cashier directed her to the back, near the washroom. She found it, dropped in her token and dialed the Lanniers' number.

El jefe et moi. The two men having dinner with Françoise. The beard, the wig.

The call from Italy. Hands reaching out for the picture. The loud laugh in her ear.

Oh, Marius, *please.*

Madame Lannier answered the phone. Ruthlessly Jessica broke into the flow of charming exclamations, and demanded Marius.

She had not really dared hope he would be there. Madame Lannier gave her the number of his office. A Saturday night, and he was working.

Oh God, thought Jessica, hanging up. Who else will she talk to?

She would have to try. At the bar, she asked for another token. They teased her for being in such a hurry.

She looked back at the door. At any moment, he would come in. His wife, he would tell them as he took her arm. You know how women are. So unreasonable. So dramatic.

Only after she dialed the office, did she realize how late it was. Certainly he would not still be there, especially on Saturday. Despair settled over her and she was starting to hang up, when she heard a click.

"Hello? Who is it?"

"Marius! That American— He's trying to kill me. It's the picture. He said—"

"Where are you, Zhessica?"

"In the Old Town. A bar. I don't know where I am. Marius, I called your home. I had to."

"Tell me where you are. I am coming."

"I don't know." A man came out of the washroom. She grabbed his sleeve. "Monsieur, *s'il vous plait*." She told Marius, "Ask him," and held the receiver to the man's ear.

There was a lengthy exchange, and then the man gave her back the telephone.

"I don't know where is this place," Marius admitted. "The Old Town, it is not so familiar. Can you leave there? Meet me at the flower market. It is covered, it will be dark. Can you find the flower market?"

"Yes, I saw it. I'm—"

He cut short her plea that she was afraid to leave the bar. "Wait at the west end of it," he said. "The end that is toward your hotel. And be careful."

Did he really need to add that? She started toward the door, nodding thank you to the cashier. The man who had talked to Marius had left.

She stood in the doorway, surveying the street. Of course she wouldn't see him. He would have ducked into another entrance. The Old Town was filled with niches, crevices, alleys—and people. He could be anywhere among all those people.

He had been wearing the tan suit again. A suit, no less. Had he really meant to take her to dinner and confront her there, and only by chance discovered she had trapped herself in the park? He must have been following her.

Or were others watching?

I'll never make it, she thought, and took a step away from the café. She began to walk toward the flower market. It would be easy to find it again. The Old Town was not large. And the market was closed now, and empty, in the middle of a broad plaza. *She* would be easy to find.

For no reason, she remembered the time on the train when he had unsuccessfully flicked his lighter. Could it have been a camera? There had been others who knew what she looked like. If he was what Weyland implied, he might very well be equipped with such sophisticated gadgetry.

Steve? The salesman from Cleveland? She could hardly believe it.

Which was the whole idea. He may not even have been American. They were good at that, too.

But was she worth the bother?

No, not she. Weyland. His formula and contacts.

She was nearly there. She could see the flower market as though through a keyhole at the end of the street.

Suddenly they blocked her way.

She whirled around. They were coming from the back, too.

Four of them. And no one, none of the people scurrying home to dinner, seemed to notice. She must not give way to panic.

Four of them. The same four. The wiry one, who could swing up to a roof. The tall one. She recognized him now, even without the mustache he had worn on his visit to Fort Sheffield with El Jefe.

They were trapping her, just like the other time when they tried to take her purse. Now they were after more than just the picture.

She feigned stupidity, pretending she did not know that she, too, was a danger.

"I don't have it," she told them loudly, and with a sharp movement, darted into the street, slipping through the tightening cordon.

The plaza was nearly empty, the flower market deserted.

She could not run. Not on cobblestones, in sandals. And they were four to her one.

She dodged into the center aisle of the market. It was dark, as he had said, but not dark enough to hide her.

One of the men followed. Two more came in from the side aisles ahead of her.

If she ran from the market, she would lose Marius and any chance of help.

If she screamed—but they could explain that to anyone who cared.

Even a bullet with a silencer. Who would notice in time that she had been shot?

She ducked under a table. She was scarcely agile in her skirt and sandals, but took them by surprise. She rolled over, passing under the table before they knew what was happening. Now she was outside the market, her dress covered with dirt.

They quickly rallied, seeming to coordinate without any sound.

"Au secours!" she cried to the passersby in the square. What did they think was going on?

A large man in blue jeans saw her and flung his arms out to the sides in distress at the unfortunate situation. A pretty girl in trouble. She ran to him, graphically clutching at her heart. *"Oh, Monsieur, au secours, s'il vous plaît."*

He answered with a stream of French. She looked back to indicate her attackers. They were nowhere in sight.

The man picked her up and threw her against a wall. She screamed.

Then she saw the danger. A screeching car had hurtled into the square and nearly run them down.

"Marius!"

A second car careened into the plaza and braked to a halt.

The police.

"Oh, Marius!"

Charles and Marius jumped from the first car and wrested her from the astonished man who still held her against the wall.

"No, no," she cried, "he helped me!" At Marius's blank expression, she tried it in French. *"Il est mon ami. Merci, monsieur. Merci!"*

In relief and gratitude she kissed the man's cheek. A happy smile spread over his face and he could settle back in contentment to watch the police write out a speeding ticket for Charles, who had been driving.

"I thought you brought them," she said to Marius, who held tightly to her arm after rescuing her from the man.

"We did bring them," he replied. "That is the quickest way to get them, no? Tell me, where is this man?"

"I don't know. There were others. The same ones who tried to grab my purse that day. They came here. How did they know?"

"They followed you. Or—" He put his hand to his forehead. *"Mon Dieu,* I have been so stupid. Come." He steered her back to the car, and Charles, and the gendarmes.

"You had better tell it to the police, what has happened. Tell them everything. And I," he added, "will back you up."

"Wait, Marius. I don't know how to say this, but you were right. I remember now. I think—El Jefe—"

"Yes. I know," he said. "I know."

22

The telephone rang, and Marius left her with his mother and Charles on the sun porch of the Lannier home. Madame Lannier held a crumpled handkerchief in her slender fingers, but did not use it. She was dry eyed, staring down the hillside at the lights of Nice.

Incredible, Jessica reflected, if not impossible. All of it. She had had good times with Steve, even though, at other times, she had found him irritating. It was still hard to imagine him as anything other than what he seemed.

Marius came back and stood in the doorway.

"Zhessica, my dear, you will be interested to know that they have got your friend. He was trying to cross into Italy. I suppose he thought you would be stopped before you could talk to the police."

"I suppose so." He had certainly tried. She added quickly, "Thanks. I'm glad."

Madame Lannier stirred, wadding the handkerchief more tightly. "And what about my friend?"

Marius gave her the news in her own language. Jessica understood that Mr. Augustín had fled and that a police bulletin had been issued, charging him with acts of sabotage and the suspicion of being a foreign operative. And Marius was correct in deducing that the telephone in his office had been bugged, as well as the one at home. That was how they had known that Jessica would be at the flower market.

Madame Lannier turned to her. "I am so sorry, Zhessica, for all of this."

"Don't be," Jessica said. The tragedy was so much worse for the older woman, who had lost a daughter, as well as her good faith in someone she had trusted and liked.

"I just couldn't understand," she went on, "why Steve kept trying to discourage me from meeting you people. I suppose he was afraid I'd run into Mr. Augustín and recognize him from that time I saw him in Fort Sheffield, even though he had a beard and dark hair then. I *thought* I'd seen him somewhere before."

"Also, I suppose," Marius said, "Steve was afraid you might give us the picture."

"Or whatever I had. He kept asking and trying to get it. I don't think he knew it was a picture, necessarily. He must have only learned that from Mr. Augustín. But probably there was a danger, if we got together, that we might start comparing notes. They didn't know how much either of us knew about what Françoise was doing."

"No, I didn't know what she was doing," Marius admitted, "but I introduced her to Claude. *I* did that, and I will have a hard time forgiving myself."

"It is not your fault, what happened," said his mother.

Jessica asked, "But didn't she already know him, if he worked at your factory?"

"No," Marius replied, "Claude asked for the job after that, when Bernard Martin died. Because of Henri, I suppose. So he could watch him."

And maybe that was why Bernard Martin had to die, Jessica thought. So Augustín could get the job. Then Françoise...If it was true that Françoise had done that...

If it was true, then Françoise, in a way, was still a dupe. She could not really have known what she was getting into. Once in, it was too late. She had to obey orders. Betray Henri. Kill her father's friend Martin. And be killed.

But she had struck the last blow, with her "el jefe"—although it might never have been seen by the right people, and might well have been seen and understood by the wrong ones.

What had made her do it? Which side was she on? Steve had said she was unreliable. Although still obeying orders, did she even then have a premonition of what might happen to her? Didn't she trust them, her dear friends and allies, and why not? Because she knew what they were like, or because, basically, she was against them? Only Françoise could give a definite answer to that, and they had destroyed her. Probably no one would ever really know just where she had stood.

Marius was asking his mother, "And now will you kindly translate for Charles what we have said, while Zhessica and I go out for some air?"

"What are you and Zhessica going to talk about?" Madame Lannier inquired.

"Only things that wouldn't interest you. I will tell you later. But you see, Charles has been very helpful, and he would like to know what is happening, so please be good enough to explain. Come, Zhessica." Marius took her arm and steered her down a flight of steps into the garden.

She did not know what was on his mind. He said nothing at all. She looked at his profile and wondered if all this was simply to tell her that he could not keep his promise to drive her to Marseilles tomorrow.

She would miss them both. And Charles, too.

"Marius, I feel so sorry for your mother."

"So do I, ever since my sister was killed. But she is a strong woman, and we will do our best to make her happy."

"You know," she said, pausing before a vine of moonflowers that bloomed whitely in the night, "it was so lovely up there in the park, before *he* came. I had a wonderful time in Nice, but it was all messed up by them. And now, just when I could really start enjoying it, I have to move on."

He turned her so that she faced him. She stood with her back against a retaining wall, the Broucard perfume she had worn mingling with a sweet flowery scent in the air.

"Why do you have to move on?" he asked.

"Well, because I won't see all of Europe if I don't get started, and I won't be able to change my reservations, and—"

"Zhessica, you are young. There is still much time to see all of Europe."

"But I can't just pop over here every weekend. This is my big trip."

"Why not stay?"

"Stay here? I'd love to, but how would I live?"

"You can live as I do, in my house. But you would not have to do all the things that I do. You would not have to go to the office every day and make the cement. You would not have to worry about the explosives in a perfume factory—but we hope that is now finished."

"How do you mean, live as you do?"

The retaining wall felt cool and scratchy. A shaft of light from inside the house fell on an oleander bush a little distance away, and far below her she could see the moving lights of a ship.

"Zhessica, I am asking you to marry me. Don't you understand?"

His face was dim in the night. Even with the illuminated bush close by, they stood in a pocket of shadows.

"Oh, Marius!" After a moment of disbelief, she wrapped her arms around his neck.

"Are you telling me yes?" he asked.

She drew away, just as he was ready to kiss her. "But what about Simone?"

He ran his finger down the side of her face. "Why do you ask about Simone?"

"I thought you were in love with her."

"With Simone? She is beautiful, yes, but I am not in love with her. She is not, as you Americans like to say, my type. Nor am I hers. She thinks I am not much fun. And furthermore, Simone is vain. She does not want anybody to marry her just because she was injured in his car. She wants someone who is devoted, and that is Charles. He can think of nothing else."

"Then—she's going to marry Charles?"

"That is their plan. And now, what about us?"

"It's funny," she said. "We've known each other only a week, but I feel as if it's much longer."

"It was a very busy week."

"Yes, as we Americans like to say, we've been through a lot together."

"You are teasing the way I speak English."

"No, really, your English is beautiful. But I guess, if I'm going to stay here, we'd better start working on my French."

"We will begin work immediately. And the words will come later." He took her hand and led her into the darkness of the garden.